The Laura and Shontay CHRONICLES

Complete Series

HOT LESBIAN EROTICA

Miranda Mars

WARNING

* * * * * * * * * * * * * * * * * * *

WANT FREE COPIES OF MY BOOKS?

Just visit my blog and download free copies of my books:
http://miranda-mars.awesomeauthors.org/

About the Publisher

4Fun Publishing, a member of **BLVNP Incorporated**, 340 S. Lemon #6200, Walnut CA 91789, info@blvnp.com / legal@blvnp.com
NOTE: Due to the highly emotional reaction of some people to works of erotic fiction, any email sent to the above address that contains foul language or religious references is automatically deleted by our anti-spam software and will not be seen. All other communications are welcome.

DISCLAIMER

The Laura and Shontay Chronicles Complete Series
Hot Lesbian Erotica

By: Miranda Mars

© **Miranda Mars 2015**
ISBN: 978-1-68030-323-0

Table of Contents

I Never Kissed A Girl Before

Catfight, Climax, Friends Again

La Chatte Noire

HOT LESBIAN EROTICA

I Never Kissed A Girl Before

THE LAURA AND SHONTAY CHRONICLES, PART 1

Miranda Mars

Life could be tiring when you were fucking your brains out day and night, it seemed, with half a dozen beautiful women, and dying to do so with half a dozen others. You could miss some sleep.

Dragging a little on her way to her office Laura glimpsed a woman she had never seen before talking with some other employees in the Project Management department, through which Laura had to pass, and indeed did pass every morning. The woman was very tall and skinny, black, clearly of African descent, but not dark, more light caramel-colored, the tone of her smooth skin falling between rich milk chocolate and glowing tawny velvet. She was very tall and very skinny, at least two inches taller than Laura, taller than either Randi or Yvette by at least an inch.

She wore a light tan pants suit, glasses with very large frames, and had her hair pulled tightly back around her head, though in back in fell nearly to her shoulders in a long pony tail, such a rare hair style for a black woman. Her hair did not appear to be so-called 'good' hair, but it wasn't wiry or kinky either; it fell naturally, and swished attractively around her long neck when she moved her head.

Laura hardly realized she was staring until she caught herself. Don't stare, she said to herself. Remember Tamara. Tamara had wanted to carve her up for lunch for such blatant staring.

But this girl did not resemble Tamara. She was not stunningly beautiful like Tamara—few women were—but Laura could see that her face was very lovely behind the huge lenses of her glasses, her eyes quick and intelligent, her mouth expressive. Very even white teeth. High forehead. Laura realized, as she tried not to stare, that this girl resembled Deshona more than anyone, and not physically either. Deshona was short, petite. Randi called her 'that dwarf.' This girl was as tall and thin as a Masai princess, though not as dark.

The resemblance to Deshona was in her icy exterior. The tall woman Laura was watching exhibited a crisp, serious, deadly serious, no-nonsense demeanor that reminded her very much of Deshona. Oh god, the fire under the ice again! Laura thought, knowing how it was a magnet to her lust. After Laura had scratched the surface with Deshona, the woman had turned into a raving, insatiable little fuck-slut. But you didn't know she would turn out like that, Laura warned herself, as she watched the new girl. This one may be cold on the outside and freezing like dead winter on the inside. You better not even think of it.

Laura tried to turn her head away. Anyway, she's marvelously, shockingly skinny. I don't even know if Jonelle was ever that skinny. Skinny and cold and intense. Laura ripped her attention away, aware that it was very hard to stop staring at her.

She passed a person in the corridor whom she knew casually and, trying to appear only mildly curious, asked who the new person was, the thin, tall one with the glasses.

"She's the new Director of Project Management. Shontay something. I don't know her last name." The woman made a dour face. "She's looks to be all of twenty-five, right? I guess the sky's the limit if you're already a director at twenty-five."

Laura smiled tightly and moved on. There were other matters to encumber her day, but through it all her mind kept drifting back to . . . fire and ice. I wonder if she burns under that glacier, she thought. Oh well. You have enough trouble without that. Just keep your eyes to yourself.

But, in spite of her efforts, a few days later she actually got caught staring.

Passing a conference room shortly after lunch, one in which she often attended meetings herself, she saw the door ajar. Shontay was holding a meeting with some of her staff.

For some reason, Laura stopped. She couldn't take her eyes off the woman. It was a mesmerizing moment, and she wondered to herself, while staring, why she was doing it. Shontay was not really beautiful in any conventional sense, though she had the regal bearing of some tribal princess. She did not dress in an alluring style. In fact, she was very tall and shockingly skinny and wore severely cut business pants suits in drab colors, black or brown, that hung in billowy swaths of cloth over her bony frame. She wore her hair pulled tightly back in a bun, from which a long, charming pony tail swung, really the only endearingly human thing about her appearance.

(She did have a nice little rump, though, the kind that stuck out and up a little the way Laura liked, though right then she was sitting on it, perched on the edge of the table and haranguing the troops.)

Her smooth, light brown face was half-concealed behind huge, oversized glasses that made her resemble an insect, though Laura could quickly see that behind the lenses there was a very appealing and interesting face. However, the face turned coldly to Laura as she was staring. Shontay had felt her eyes, as people often did they were being looked at, though no one knew why. She glowered at Laura, who quickly looked away, feeling her face flush hotly as she turned and walked off.

Oh god, Laura thought. Oh shit, why did I do that?

She took some consolation in the fact that it wasn't as bad as when Tamara had caught her staring, and had promptly reproached her. But she had wanted to fuck Tamara, which Tamara had known. And, Laura now knew, Tamara had secretly relished the idea, somewhere in her secret being. But this Shontay Something was not even physically appealing to Laura. She was almost sexless, as well as imperious and condescending. I don't want to . . . do it with her, Laura reasoned. It's not the same as with Tamara. But why did I stop to stare at her?

For the next few days, she did everything she could to avoid the areas of the building where she knew she would be likely to encounter Shontay. At least she would give the woman time to forget what had happened. Maybe Shontay had forgotten it already. After all, Laura thought, I could've just been standing there abstracted, thinking, pondering something. She didn't have to think I was staring at her. I wasn't, really. It didn't really have anything to do with her. Maybe it was the sound of her voice or something.

***

A few weeks passed. At work Laura kept her distance from places where she might run into Shontay. No need to resurrect that little awkward moment of The Staring in the poor thing's mind. Sure, I looked. She is . . . intriguing. But I've got my plate full already. I don't want her. Anyway, she's . . . god, is she skinny!

But then, one evening as she returned from work and stopped to check her mailbox in the lobby, she was surprised to find, just closing and locking the mailbox a few spaces down from her own . . . Shontay Something.

They both recognized one another at once. It had been a few weeks since Shontay had caught Laura inadvertently staring at her, and Laura had taken pains since then to avoid any place where they might meet. And so, at this moment, it was very difficult for her to suppress a wildly embarrassing blush.

"Say, don't you work at Hanford Carpenter, down at 333 Market?" Shontay asked. She snapped her fingers, trying to remember. "Laura . . . Laura something, isn't it?"

Laura broke into a grin. "Well, at least we have the same name. Laura. Laura Robbins." She extended her hand. "I always think of you as 'Shontay Something'."

Shontay smiled. She was, for the moment at least, not nearly as icy and aloof as she often appeared at work. "Shontay Gibson."

She shook Laura's hand. Laura looked down at Shontay's graceful, beautifully-shaped hand. Shontay was not dark like Dawn or

Charise (or even as dark as Lila, over whom Laura had now been mooning for days) but more a rich caramel color, and her long fingers clasping Laura's hand were tapered and sinuous.

"Are you living here now?" Laura asked, now opening her own mailbox. "I mean, I've lived here for a while and never seen you before."

"Oh no," Shontay laughed and shook her head. "Apartment sitting. My parents live here. Ninth floor."

Laura's eyes widened. She had never felt so stupid. Of course. *Gibson.* "You're the *Gibsons'* daughter? They're in the apartment right above mine."

As soon as she said it, she wondered if she should have. Since Kendra and Jane had moved out and the Gibsons in, she had tried to be on her best behavior about making uncontrollable rutting noises with her girlfriends. But she knew she and Jane and probably a few others had let their guard fall a few times, and she had never known, of course, if anyone had been home in the Gibsons' apartment during those outbursts. For all she knew, they had told their daughter that a lesbian lived downstairs who was always screaming away in loud ecstasy with her various lovers.

She peered through the huge lenses of the oversized glasses that Shontay always wore, trying to see if there was some spark of recognition there. *Oh, the noisy lesbian!* Something like that. But she saw nothing but Shontay's light brown eyes, so pale brown that they looked almost green, very beautiful and in a way electric and alluring, though somewhat obscured by the glossy reflections glancing off the large lenses.

"What a coincidence," Shontay said, Laura thought somewhat uneasily.

Now Laura had collected her mail, and they walked slowly together toward the elevators. Though she had always found Shontay vaguely attractive, in spite of her painful thinness and her apparently very cold nature, Laura was relieved to find that she was not urgently drawn to the girl in any way and could leave well enough alone. Not such a good thing to be making a pass at your neighbor's daughter, she told herself. After all, you already did that once, with Jane. It so happens they lived in the same apartment. We will make sure history doesn't repeat itself this time.

Shontay of course helped matters by being almost wholly asexual. Today she was wearing her loose-hanging (because of her tall, bony frame) light brown business suit, in contrast to the identical black one she wore on alternate days. Once Laura had glimpsed her in an ivory-colored one, exactly the same. She seemed to have found one sexless garment and then cloned it in different drab colors until her closet was full.

Under the suit she wore a conservative white silk blouse, and around her throat a string of pearls. She had a long, exquisite neck. Actually, she looked elegant in a 'corporate' way. Today the pony tail she often wore, which seemed to soften her features and her aloofness a little, was absent, tucked up behind her head in a bun. Laura, incorrigible as ever, managed to sneak a peek at her cute little butt as they entered the elevator together and found it as wonderful as she remembered, high, jutting. She could, however, only imagine what it must really look like under the limp swaths of cloth that hid it.

Elevators made everyone uncomfortable, Laura knew. Shontay broke the silence, almost perfunctorily, gazing abstractedly up at the ceiling as she spoke.

"My mother has this cat. She's afraid it will be lonely. They're down in Mazatlan, at a conference and vacation add-on. So . . . I'm taking care of Willie, that's the cat. And staying there for a few days."

Laura was so glad, as the elevator reached the eighth floor, that she didn't feel a desperate urge to get into Shontay's pants. She's okay, but gosh is she skinny, she thought, repeating herself, as if chanting a soft, exculpatory mantra. She smiled at Shontay.

"Well, if I can be of any help, just let me know. I'll be right downstairs. You can even stamp on the floor to get my attention."

Shontay gave her a genuinely friendly grin, so friendly that Laura realized she herself must have been exaggerating the incident where she had thought Shontay had caught her staring. Maybe it had not even been noticed.

"I will. Take care."

Laura smiled as the elevator doors slid shut.

In her apartment, she promptly forgot about Shontay, feeling for once very proud of this demonstration of her self-mastery. Instead, she fell to thinking about Lila again, and Dawn. There was certainly enough emotional turmoil in her sex life to keep her occupied, and she didn't need to go falling again for that melt-the-ice-cube challenge she had already gone through with Deshona. She had not seen Deshona either for months now, and that brought her a fresh set of pains.

Reading her mail, drinking a glass of wine, watching a little of the news on TV, she lost track of time. When her phone rang, she reached for it distractedly.

"Is this Laura . . . Laura Robbins?"

She recognized Shontay's voice. "Yes. Shontay?"

"I didn't know how to spell your name. Whether it had one 'b' or two."

"Yes, it's me. Is something wrong?"

"Oh no. I was just . . . fixing something to eat. The idea of eating it all alone . . . or just with Willie . . . didn't seem too hot. I wondered if you wanted to come up and eat dinner here. You know, it's kind of lonely in this big old apartment."

Laura felt a tiny acceleration of the pulse in her neck. She had done her best not to think about Shontay in a sexual way, which was not hard since Shontay wasn't very attractive. Too skinny and remote. But now she could easily recognize a hot, feathery little excitement in her body that meant her interest was awakening. Could she turn the invitation down?

"I . . . haven't eaten yet. I guess I could," she heard herself saying.

"Good," Shontay sounded relieved. "I'll see you in a few seconds."

"Are we 'dressing' for dinner?" Laura joked, suddenly wondering if that sounded too risqué.

"Wear what you've got on. Willie won't care, and I won't notice."

"Be right there."

Laura went to the mirror and combed her hair and washed her face, so that she would appear more fresh and vibrant, feeling a little end-of-day fatigue. She blinked and scrutinized her eyes. Do I look like a sexual predator? she wondered. Well, I won't be. This is just a friendly dinner.

She tried on several causal smiles, then, dissatisfied with any of them, resolved to be warm, relaxed, and . . . what? Neighborly. At the last minute, before going out the door, she decided to bring along a bottle of wine.

Upstairs Shontay met her at the door, holding Willie in her arms. Willie was a white Persian, with startling pale blue eyes. She had changed out of the severe business suit and was now wearing black jeans and a faded red sweatshirt. She had removed the pearl necklace from her exquisite neck, too. Most noticeable to Laura, however, was the fact that Shontay's hair, always so primly combed and pulled back tightly, was now loose around her face, falling nearly to her shoulders.

Laura held out the wine. "My little contribution."

Shontay smiled, closing the door behind them. "Let's go see if we can find a corkscrew. My Mom and Dad don't drink." She raised her eyebrows sarcastically. "Their only vice is overwork."

They could not find one, and Laura had to go back downstairs to get one of hers. When she returned, they shared a glass of wine at sat by the window. The view was identical to Laura's but somehow seemed fresh, since the furniture was different, and she suddenly felt herself being attracted to Shontay in a way that she had not been before. She felt it even more so when Shontay removed her glasses, placing huge frames and lenses on a nearby lamp table and revealing a face that now seemed smaller, more proportional to the rest of her body, and very lovely, though still in a cold, remote way.

But now Laura could see her eyes better. They were light brown, almost green, and made her stare somehow electric and unusual.

"Why are you looking at me that way?" she asked Laura.

"Your eyes, I guess. I . . . don't think I noticed them, really, until you took off your glasses. They're stunning."

Shontay looked annoyed. "You think so? Maybe that's why I wear the glasses all the time."

"You don't like having beautiful eyes?"

Shontay gave her a curt smile. "They're odd. That's all. Big deal. How long have you been working at Hanford Carpenter?"

"About five years now."

"How can you stand it?"

Laura was mildly startled. Shontay was a newcomer to the company, but—as gossips had nastily asserted—she was only about twenty-five and had been hired in as a Director. It had taken Laura over four years to be made Director. Shontay was smart, attractive, aggressive, completely in charge, and could look forward to a very rewarding career.

She saw Laura's puzzlement.

"I mean, there's so much politics . . . so much devious political maneuvering. Don't you find it suffocating?"

This was always dangerous territory, talking with someone you barely knew about job politics.

"Oh, I guess I just wiggle my way through the sharks with a little smile that says 'Don't eat me, please'," Laura laughed uncomfortably.

"Do you mind if I smoke?" Shontay asked abruptly. "I mean, I'm not supposed to in their place, but if I air it out before they get back, maybe they won't know."

Laura smiled. "I don't mind. It's your neck, not mine. Your parents too."

Shontay crossed the room to her purse and took out a pack of cigarettes. Laura could not help letting her eyes linger on the girl's long legs and pretty ass, so much more apparent now that she was wearing jeans that fit her more tightly than the limp business suit pants had.

Again she marveled at how tall Shontay was. She was skinny-shanked, long, and lithe, but her curvaceous little rump stuck out when she walked.

After a brief trip to the kitchen for a saucer to use as an ashtray, Shontay returned and lit a cigarette with a brief, brusque, almost angry flourish. She was very angular and intense, Laura noticed. In fact, Laura had noticed it before, though only from a distance, and it had been one of the things that put her off. Now it only made her uncomfortable and wary.

"They hate it that I smoke," Shontay said, exhaling two long streams of smoke from her nostrils. "Anyway, I've only been there a few months, but I could sure tell you some of the sharks to avoid. Like that imperious bitch Rhonda Reardon for one." She looked at Laura for a reaction. "Maybe I shouldn't say anything," she said, looking away, taking a deep drag. "You and she are probably friends."

Laura was amused. "Did you have a little run-in with dear Rhonda?"

"What a cunt! Excuse me, I did it again."

"She and I are hardly friends," Laura said, delighted to have a way to ingratiate herself at Rhonda's expense. "She *is* a little hard to take sometimes."

If you only knew, darling Shontay, how she probably goes home at night and just dreams of pushing her face up between your long, skinny, brown thighs.

Shontay scowled. It was clear that just the thought of Rhonda about ruined her evening. That's fine, Laura thought, since I feel the same way. Let's change the subject.

They talked for a while about other things, but Shontay continued to be tense and sharp and her conversation full of treacherous angles that Laura preferred to avoid. After one glass of wine, they went to the kitchen, where Laura helped her make a salad. It was a small kitchen, identical to Laura's downstairs, and Laura was used to maneuvering around in it, but Shontay was not. While Laura was leaning down to replace something in the refrigerator, Shontay passed behind her, and when Laura stood, they collided.

"Oh shit!" Shontay said, dropping the knife she had been holding. "Look out!"

The tip of the knife grazed the knee of Laura's pants but did not cut through the cloth. The knife clattered to the floor. They both watched it, and when they looked up found themselves staring into each other's eyes, their faces very close, Shontay's hand on Laura's shoulder, and Laura's on Shontay's hip. For a moment it was as if they were caught in a freeze-frame, not moving, not breathing.

"Did it get you?" Shontay murmured the question.

"No," Laura murmured back.

Their eyes were locked. This girl is lovely, Laura found herself thinking, enchanted by the unusual soft billowing of hair around Shontay's face. She let her eyes drop to Shontay's mouth, which she purposely had not examined closely until now. Shontay's lips were full and curved and sensual. I want to kiss them, Laura thought. I want to devour them.

She looked back up into Shontay's mysterious pale brown eyes, hoping to see a warning there. *You'd better not try it*, something like that. But Shontay seemed paralyzed too.

Usually Laura had good self-control, but now she was unable to stop herself from leaning her head just a few inches more forward, tilting her face up—since Shontay was a good two inches taller than she—until her own lips brushed Shontay's. She moved her mouth slowly back and forth, letting their lips brush but not actually kissing the girl. Shontay did not move. Then she said,

"What are you doing?"

She did not raise her voice, but her stare did not flinch either. Laura stared back, trying to equal the steely force in Shontay's mesmerizing eyes. But it was very hard to control her anxiety at having made a huge mistake.

"I . . . don't know," she said, her outward calm concealing a wild turbulence inside. She pulled her head back. "I just . . . wanted to. Something about you just made me want to."

Shontay had not smiled throughout the encounter. She still did not smile. Her face was cold and suspicious. Finally, she seemed to relax a little, dropping her shoulders, which neither of them had realized were elevated until she lowered them. Laura realized that she too was tense and tried to relax.

Shontay bent down to pick up the knife. "So . . . you like girls?"

Laura's eyes were on the knife. Shontay saw her looking at it. A large, uncontrollable grin spread over her face.

She lay the knife down on the butcher block table next to them. "Don't worry," she half-laughed, "it's safe to tell me. Nothing worth killing over."

Laura played nervously with her fingers, smiling back now. "I'm sorry. I apologize. Something about the moment . . . I was looking into those wonderful eyes of yours . . . and we were so close . . . I could smell your perfume . . . I just gave in to the impulse."

A flicker of amusement and pleasure now began to dance in Shontay's eyes. She, like anyone, enjoyed being praised, enjoyed the thought that something about her had been irresistible to Laura. But she felt the need to taunt Laura further.

"You didn't answer my question."

Laura could see the steel flashing again. "Now I see why they made you a director when you were hired."

"Well, it wasn't any affirmative action bullshit, if that's what you're implying," Shontay snapped.

Laura was floored. "I wasn't implying anything. I think you're very . . . self-possessed."

She turned and walked out of the kitchen. You and Rhonda would be a good match, she thought, trying to get control of her feelings. Two of a kind.

Momentarily, but not immediately, Shontay followed her. She seemed conciliatory. Laura was gazing out the window at the view, the same one she could see from her own apartment. She acted as if she were alone when Shontay joined her there.

They both looked at the view, silently. They could hear one another's breathing.

"You don't have to answer it," Shontay finally said, softly.

Laura turned to her. "I . . . just wanted to do it," she repeated. "I couldn't help it. I can go now, if you like."

Shontay looked down, embarrassed, and Laura suddenly realized that the girl had been excited by the brushing of their lips, and she didn't want Laura to go but didn't know how to say otherwise.

"I . . . I can't eat all that salad myself," she half-whispered. "It'll just get rotten. Willie doesn't eat salad." She grinned.

Suddenly, and for the first time, Laura felt an overpowering lust for Shontay, a true, hot, physical craving for her body, painfully skinny though it might be. She wanted to enfold the girl, and break through the ice shield into the quivering vulnerability inside. If I stay, Laura thought, I won't be able to ignore this feeling. Better to let it all out at once, better to risk it now than later.

"I want to do that again. What we did in the kitchen," she said softly, boldly, letting her eyes dive deep into Shontay's pale brown miracles.

Shontay shook her head ever so slightly. "I don't think so."

"Why not?"

Now Shontay's embarrassed look became even more acute. She realized it and turned away from Laura, even moving a few steps back from the window.

"I just . . . don't go for it is all. I just don't do that. With men either. It's just not my thing."

Laura pursued her. She felt that she had no choice, and she moved a few more steps toward Shontay. Finally she was as close to her as they had been by the window. Laura reached out and caressed her smooth light brown cheek.

"Your skin is so smooth," she whispered.

She let her finger move around to Shontay's mouth, turning it so that the knuckle slid tenderly across the girl's sensual lips. Shontay seemed hypnotized by this tenderness, which was exactly Laura's intent. She could almost feel the yearning inside the girl, fighting to get out of the ice cage that entrapped it.

Abruptly, Shontay turned her head away, then turned her whole body and walked away without a word, returning to the kitchen. Laura did not follow her. She needs to be alone with those feelings for a minute, she reasoned. Whatever they are. Laura found Willie and began stroking him, making friends. Willie purred like a love-starved tractor and rubbed the side of his head violently against Laura's hand.

After a few minutes had passed, she went into the kitchen. It was remarkable how not talking, not facing one another for a brief interval could alter the mood again. Shontay was brisk and indifferent, as if Laura had never brushed her lips with her own. Laura fell right into the mood and picked up the salad bowl, moving it to the small dining table on the other side of the counter top.

"Another glass of wine?" she asked.

Shontay smiled. It was a very different smile from any she had given Laura before, somehow more intimate, warmer. We kissed, Laura thought. It was only a little brush of the lips, but she knows we kissed. That's what she's smiling about.

She poured each of them another glass of wine. Shontay had still not moved from the kitchen toward the table. Laura waited. Shontay turned and looked at her.

"You really want to do that again?" she asked, so softly that Laura almost could not hear her.

Laura's heart fluttered. Yes!

She walked calmly around the counter and back into the kitchen. "Yes," she whispered, looking dreamily up into the electrifying pale brown eyes. "But you're so tall . . . you'll have to stoop down a little."

"I don't mind that," Shontay whispered back. "No touching, though."

"No touching," Laura shook her head.

Their eyes were locked in a pulsing connection as they brought their faces close, then closer. Shontay bent her head down slightly. Their lips brushed again, as before. As promised, Laura kept her hands at her sides, letting her lips express everything she felt. First she lightly brushed Shontay's with them as before.

Their eyes were still open, still looking at each other, though too close to really see anything but skin and facial contours. Laura could almost taste Shontay's sweet, moist breath. Shontay did little but let Laura's lips caress hers. She didn't move or blink.

Laura slowly pressed closer. She pressed her lips into Shontay's marvelously sensual mouth, tilting her head to let them curve naturally into the receptive curvature of Shontay's own lips, finally feeling a slow awakening, a responsive movement in Shontay's mouth against hers. Now they were really kissing, not flirting with it, and Laura saw Shontay's eyelids fall, feeling an almost palpable warmth that had not been there before begin to radiate between their bodies, which were still separated by about six inches.

Moved and aroused by this warmth, and by Shontay's pliant, yielding mouth, Laura barely realized that she had raised her hand and let her fingertips run very gently across Shontay's cheek. But Shontay opened her eyes.

"No touching," she said softly. "You promised."

Laura dropped her hand. "You're right. I did. I forgot."

Now they had broken off the kiss and needed to start it again. Shontay looked at Laura, unwilling to resume it herself. Laura smiled and moved her mouth back into the position it had occupied when Shontay had spoken, now for the first time flicking just the tip of her tongue into the crease formed by Shontay's closed lips. Surprisingly,

Shontay parted them a little, not enough to let Laura's tongue slip inside, but enough to encourage her.

Ever patient, her hot blood beginning to surge through her body, Laura teased Shontay's half-parted lips with the tip of her tongue, expressively moving her mouth against them too. She tried to communicate telepathically with the girl, beaming her feelings at Shontay, reassuring her, verbally caressing her too, but silently. *I think you are so lovely, Shontay . . . so much lovelier than I had thought . . . so soft and luminous now with your hair down around your face . . . so afraid of a little warmth and so scared of your feelings. I would just love to kiss every bit of you . . . all of your long, smooth body. Wouldn't you like me to do that? Wouldn't you like me, for example, to kiss you between your thighs? Wouldn't you like me to kiss that pretty little bottom of yours? Would you let me? I could make you feel so good.*

This kiss had now gone on quite a while, and Laura marveled that neither of them grew impatient enough to push it further, or in Shontay's case, perhaps, to break it off. *She likes it*, Laura realized. She pushed a little harder with her tongue, trying to get it inside Shontay's mouth. Almost imperceptibly, Shontay's full lips parted more, then even more, and soon Laura's tongue was sliding in past her teeth.

This was a penetration of sorts, and both of them knew it. Laura could even feel a faint, very faint shudder in Shontay as she felt Laura's tongue enter her mouth. Her own tongue did not meet Laura's. Passive and yielding, she did nothing to stop Laura's probing tongue, though Laura could feel her breathing accelerate.

After about half a minute, Shontay slowly pulled back, breaking off the kiss. She was breathing more heavily, her eyes slightly glassy. She gave Laura a tight, nervous smile.

"I liked that," Laura breathed, smiling back. "Let's sit down and do some more of it."

Without nodding or making any other sign of assent, Shontay walked slowly into the living room, with Laura following. They sat down together on the sofa. Now Shontay's mysterious pale brown eyes were glowing, throbbing, dreamy.

Laura raised a tentative hand, as if to caress her smooth cheek again. "Still no touching?" she asked.

Shontay shook her head. "No touching," she croaked softly, betraying a physical excitement Laura knew she was trying to conceal.

Laura shrugged and smiled. "Okay."

As long as I can kiss you, I'll agree not to touch you. Laura leaned close, but this time before pressing her mouth into Shontay's, she let her lips skim the side of her cheek, then slid them down her jaw to her long, brown, swan's neck, so smooth and flawless. Laura kissed the delectable smooth column slowly, with great tenderness, down to the beautiful curved shallow indentation of Shontay's throat, then back up under her chin, until her lips again arrived at Shontay's mouth.

Now when they kissed again, even Shontay was more excited. She mingled her half-open lips with Laura's more ardently than before, letting Laura's tongue inside more quickly this time, even meeting it with her own. It became very hard for Laura to kiss her but not touch her.

"Can I touch you?" she panted softly.

"No," Shontay shook her head.

"Why?"

Laura kissed her neck again, the other side, waiting for an answer. Shontay was panting now, too. But she shook her head again with determination.

"I gave this up," she responded, after a moment's pause. "I mean, you know, sex."

She pulled back to look at Laura. Her eyes showed her sexual excitement, but her mouth was now pinched and cold and grim, the way Laura had often seen it at work. She looked exasperated, as if there were no way to get out of owing Laura an explanation, since they had gone at least this far.

"I never . . . liked it." She looked away, out the window. "So I quit. I've been happier since I gave it up."

Laura said nothing. She didn't know what to say. Shontay looked back to see Laura's puzzled, sympathetic expression.

"Never like this, of course. I never kissed a girl . . . until you. But guys, yes. A few. I'm so tall . . . a lot of them won't say 'boo' to me. But I did it . . . with a few tall guys. I never . . . really had a climax with any of them. And they were jerks. So I figured, why keep it up? I can be fine without it."

She gave Laura a tight smile.

"You never came at all?"

Shontay shook her head. "By myself . . ." her voice trailed off.

"By yourself you can?" Laura asked gently, trying not to be too pushy.

Shontay nodded.

Laura shrugged. "I love kissing you," she confessed softly. "We don't have to do anything else. You like it, don't you?"

Shontay grinned, embarrassed. She nodded. "I do."

"Let's do some more."

"Okay."

They had another long, expressive, exploratory kiss. Shontay allowed herself to get deeper into it this time, coiling tongues with Laura, kissing back. While they were kissing, Laura got an idea. She didn't spring it on Shontay immediately, being too overjoyed at this moving kiss, and Shontay's growing warmth. But when they stopped, she kissed Shontay's ear, her earlobe, her neck again, giving her the excited shivers.

"Ooohhhh . . . you're tickling me," she giggled.

"I have an idea. If you don't like it, just say so and we'll drop it." Laura smiled. "I'm enjoying this too much to stop it if you don't like my idea."

"What is it?"

Laura blushed a little even to say it. Her face suffused with rosey tinges, but her embarrassment seemed to charm Shontay, who leaned closer, as if to encourage her.

"Why don't we just lie down together and each do it ourselves? And we could kiss . . . we wouldn't have to touch any more than that. I'd really like to do it with you that way. I mean, it's not really like we're doing it. Just kissing, you know, while we do it alone."

This was very perverse reasoning, but Laura thought Shontay might be excited, and titillated, enough to swallow it. She might want to go through with it if Laura made it sound tempting enough. But Shontay just kept staring at her, as if in disbelief.

"How about it?" Laura prompted, losing hope quickly.

Shontay shook her head. "I gave it up," she said again, softly. "It's nothing against you. I . . . even like you."

She said it as if she could not understand why. Laura, in spite of the prohibition, again ran a fingertip along her cheek to her lips.

"May I keep kissing you?"

Shontay gave her the curt smile again. "Maybe we'd better not."

"One last kiss?"

Shontay tilted her head. Again her pleasure at being so sexually attractive to Laura was transparently obvious. She nodded.

This time their kiss, though it began slowly, became even hotter than the last one. Shontay was sending Laura very mixed messages. Not content to offer her open mouth to Laura, now she slid her own tongue back into Laura's mouth too, her lips searching, her tongue probing, her warm yearning very clear. It was an agony for Laura not to touch her as their mouths entangled in a hungry, aggressive kiss, hungrier by the moment.

Finally, they had to break it off before they incinerated one another. Both were half-dazed by the intensity of it. Shontay looked at Laura oddly, as she had before in the kitchen.

"You really want to do that?"

Laura smiled and nodded slowly. "I think I would come in only a few seconds if I were kissing you," she whispered, her eyes smoking with meaning.

"I . . . guess we could try it," Shontay said, tentatively.

Laura reached out and took her hand. Somehow it seemed to her as if they were moving under water as they slowly rose together from the sofa and walked in slow motion, still holding hands, toward the master bedroom. Since the floor plan of this apartment was identical to Laura's own, she could have found the bedroom in her sleep, and indeed it did seem as if she and Shontay were sleepwalking as they floated, glided, and sailed airily down the short hallway.

Only as they went through the doorway did Laura realize—and she knew Shontay did, too—that they were going to undergo this potentially marvelous experience in the bed of Shontay's parents. The bedroom, so familiar in its contours, felt at the same time very alien to Laura since it was furnished in a completely different taste, with golden draperies and French baroque furniture.

Fortunately, she and Shontay were still at least half-sunk in the sleepwalking mode, and together they peeled back the bedspread from the queen-sized bed, then turned on the small lamps on each bedstand. It was all so neat and clean and somehow elegant, and Laura could feel sexual excitement trembling deep inside her belly as she looked up to see Shontay's pale brown eyes glimmering and shiny, full of fascination mingled with a sexual allure that she probably didn't even know was there.

Laura went around to the other side of the bed and took her hand again. She encouraged Shontay to sit down on the edge of it with her, knowing how uncomfortable she must be, and knowing that they just couldn't stand there across from one another in Shontay's mother's bedroom and start stripping off their clothes.

"Lie back with me here and give me another kiss," she murmured, gently pulling Shontay down on the bed, face to face with her. "No touching," she added, partly as a little wry joke between them, which, Laura could see from the twinkle of her eye, Shontay caught.

They kissed, much more seriously now that they were lying together on a bed, where something definitely would happen. When they finally stopped, Shontay for the first time lifted her own hand to Laura's face and touched Laura's lips with her fingertip.

"How does it feel to have all that hair?" she asked, softly.

Laura had begun to unbutton the front of her own shirt, and she paused, sitting up, shaking her hair self-consciously. She remembered how, long ago, another girl had asked her the same question.

"Feels like I'm a lioness," she purred.

"Lionesses don't have manes," Shontay said. "The males do."

"Well . . . I'm not one of them," Laura said, finally undoing the last button.

Her shirt came open, revealing her black lace bra, cut low on her breasts, a very enticing one. She had not put it on specially for this but had worn it to work and just not removed it yet. But Shontay's eyes went to it immediately.

"No . . . you're not," she said.

Slowly, realizing this was a bargain, she began to pull her own faded red sweatshirt up over her head. Laura watched her smooth, rich, creamy caramel skin come into view, her lean stomach and waist, the nicely-defined cambers of her ribcage as she lifted the sweatshirt over her head and patted her hair back down. She wore a simple white bra, but Laura was delightfully surprised to see that it contained actual breasts, small but definitely there, round and bulging.

From looking at Shontay fully-clothed, you would have to guess that she was flat-chested, but actually she even had cleavage, and though very thin and a little bony, as Laura had expected, she was well-formed. The bones of her shoulders and her clavicles did not protrude in awkward angles but were sculptured and fine, and Laura realized that, though it might be a matter of taste, this thin, starved-model look was not totally without appeal. Shontay in only her bra was very lovely.

She also appeared more vulnerable to Laura than ever. Gone was the abrupt, sharp sarcasm and dour wit, even the aloof, remote scorn that was so apparent in her manner at work, and, even though she had moderated it, in her bearing when she had met Laura down at the mailboxes in the lobby. It was hard to be imperious and distant when you were in your underwear, about to share an intimate physical moment with someone you had never imagined you would do this with only an hour ago.

Laura smiled warmly at her. She unzipped her own jeans and began to slip out of them. As if hypnotized and only following the leader, Shontay began to do the same with her black jeans. Laura could not keep her eyes away from Shontay's long, skinny legs coming into view as the girl pulled her jeans down. She saw Laura's eyes on them and became self-conscious.

"My legs are pretty skinny," she apologized.

They *were* pretty skinny, Laura had to agree, and immensely long, but Laura found them very attractive, not really sticks of bone, as she had anticipated, but thin and shapely and smooth, with a glowing, almost mahogany sheen that made her want to press her lips to Shontay's shins, and her supple calves, and her elongated but satiny thighs. Oh god, I want to fuck you more than ever now, Laura thought, letting her eyes communicate it to Shontay since their eyes frequently locked and throbbed together.

"I think they're beautiful," Laura murmured. "If it weren't for 'no touching,' I would kiss them."

"You would?"

"Yes."

Now they both wore only their panties and their bras. Using both hands, Laura lifted her hair off her back, then turned it to Shontay.

"You help me . . . then I'll help you."

Shontay obediently unfastened Laura's bra. Laura slid the straps off her arms. She turned back, seeing Shontay's eyes fall to her naked breasts, then rise again quickly, as if she were unwilling to let Laura see that she was interested.

"Now you," Laura prompted softly.

Shontay looked at her, expressionless. After this garment was gone, there would be only one more apiece. Then they would be naked. Laura wondered if Shontay were having misgivings. On the other hand, when you had gone this far, it was hard to go back.

A small, ambiguous smile tugged up only one corner of Shontay's mouth. Her hair did not fall far enough to obscure her bra clasp, and so she merely turned her back to Laura and waited. It was an enchanting back, which Laura had not really seen until now. It was long, incredibly long, smooth, a rich, warm brown in color. I could spend a year just kissing this back, Laura realized as she slowly unfastened Shontay's bra. And she won't let me touch it.

Impetuously, she asked, in a soft, sultry murmur, trying not to seem too seductive. "Shontay . . . you have such a beautiful back. Are you sure I can't just touch it . . . or kiss it . . . just for a second?"

Shontay grinned back over her shoulder, as if she had known that once Laura had seen her back it would be endless love. Of course, Laura reflected, one rarely knew how beautiful one's back actually was, if indeed it was. Instead, Shontay was giving in to a coquettish impulse, of all things.

"You know the rules," Shontay said, eyes flashing with mischief.

Laura's face collapsed in disappointment. Shontay turned to her, slowly removing her own limp bra now. A subtle shift had taken place in her mood. She seemed delighted that Laura was so captivated by her body and was well aware that if Laura liked her legs and her back, she had a more surprising treat coming.

Shontay's small breasts were exquisite little round balls of firm flesh, not mere swellings, as Laura had expected, having slept with Jonelle, who had been surely as skinny as Shontay when they had first been together. They were small enough so that when she wore a silk blouse under a business suit, her chest appeared completely flat, but actually they were the size of tea cups, almost perfectly round, with soft, dark brown nipples the size of quarters, a slightly deeper shade of caramel from the rest of her lovely long body.

Laura was overcome by a craving to hold them, to kiss them, to suck them hungrily and make love to them painstakingly. And she knew Shontay could see it. Her expression said: *I knew you'd like these. See what I mean? It always surprises people that I've got these little gems.*

"God, they're beautiful," Laura said in a whisper.

Shontay looked down at her own naked breasts, feigning interest, as if her attention had been called to them for the first time. "You think so?"

Laura nodded.

"I wish I had bigger ones . . . like yours."

Laura could not suppress a giggle. It was rare that her breasts were bigger than anybody's. "Would it be 'touching' if we just . . . sort of, you know . . . pushed them together for a second? Just to see what it feels like?"

Shontay gave her another prim but coquettish smile. "I think we better stick to the rules."

But this time Laura could sense that Shontay now had acknowledged that this was a sort of game, and the outcome was still uncertain. Laura was willing to play along. Again she drew Shontay down beside her, face to face. They were still both wearing their panties.

"I want to kiss you again before we go on," she whispered.

Shontay smiled slowly. "I want you to know I'm really enjoying this," she half-breathed, very softly, almost inaudibly, as if hoping neither one of them would hear it.

"Good. Me too. I especially like kissing you. Your mouth is . . . so warm, so sweet. I love it."

Shontay squinted. "I kind of like yours too."

They kissed, very tenderly now. Again it was agony for Laura not to touch her. Shontay's tongue entered Laura's mouth this time before Laura had a chance to be first, and it made Laura's heart flutter all over again. She realized that she was very wet and wondered if Shontay was too. How could she not be? Laura thought. God, this is so exciting.

"You know, honey," she panted against Shontay's half-open lips, "if we don't get on with it, I think I'm going to come just from this."

Again Shontay was curious. "Really?"

Laura nodded. "I'm pretty wet. Aren't you?"

Shontay nodded. "Yes. Let's do it."

They disengaged their lips and slowly pulled their panties down and off. Their eyes never unlocked, and they could hear every rustle, every creak of the bed springs, every soft hiss of their naked skin sliding against the sheet, as they each slowly skimmed their panties down their legs and kicked them free of their ankles. Now they were completely naked, facing one another side by side on the bed, their mouths just inches apart.

Laura reached down with one hand to her crotch, parting her thighs, feeling the moisture in her pubic patch, the overflow from a wildly aroused cunt, which was throbbing and pulsing madly. Not wanting to be too obvious, she tried not to look directly as Shontay's hand descended too. Instead, she pushed her head forward again until her lips met Shontay's.

"Kiss me . . . Shontay," she breathed.

"Yes," Shontay sighed.

She bit her lower lip, and her eyes rolled up as she touched herself. Laura slid two fingers into the warm, buttery folds of her own pussy, feeling her whole body stream and glow with fire. Imperceptibly, almost as if they were sharing a dream, Laura could feel the whole atmosphere change as the two of them actually began to masturbate, slowly at first, but, in Laura's case, quickly accelerating. She wanted to go slowly, to give things a chance to develop, but as her tongue intermingled with Shontay's, and their hot, rapid breath filled the air around their searching mouths, she found herself rubbing her wet pussy more and more frantically, unable to stop herself from hurtling toward a thrilling climax.

"Oh!" she heard her own voice, softly gasping. "Oh! Oh . . . yes!"

Shontay's eyes rolled up again. Laura let her gaze travel down the girl's long, smooth, light-brown body. They stopped at Shontay's beautiful little breasts, the size of tea cups, jiggling and bouncing slightly now as she swirled her hand in her crotch, her deep caramel brown nipples winking out at Laura from behind Shontay's elbow or forearm as her arm moved. Oh god, I want her! Laura thought in a rush of desperate lust.

"Ummmm! Unnhhh!" Shontay groaned softly. "Laura . . ."

"Yes . . . yes, honey," Laura panted. "Oh, it's so good to do this with you. Kiss me!"

"Unhhh! Ohhhh!"

They writhed and squirmed, only inches from touching, their mouths moving hungrily together, their tongues dancing and stabbing more passionately now, their panting quickly modulating into an uncontrollable mewling as they both became more and more aroused. Breaking the rules, but almost without knowing it, Laura raised her free hand to Shontay's cheek, brushing back the black filaments of her soft hair and letting her fingertips graze the perfect, smooth skin.

"I want you . . . I want you," she panted, kissing Shontay more aggressively now, unable to hold herself back.

Shontay's pale brown eyes were now streaked by fierce sexual need, an expression Laura had never seen there before. She began to respond to Laura's feverish kissing more heatedly, opening her mouth wider, pushing her tongue further into Laura's mouth, whimpering now, writhing and shaking, moving her own hand faster, as Laura could tell from the way her elbow jumped and rotated.

"Oh . . . Jesus!" Shontay gasped, her eyelids fluttering.

"Shontay . . . I want you, I've got to touch you!" Laura panted. "You are so beautiful. Let me touch you . . . please!"

Shontay's eyes fluttered open, glassy, burning with sexual fever, telegraphing a message to Laura that all resistance was fading fast, that she was sinking and would not try to prevent anything Laura decided to do. Laura pressed her advantage quickly, not know how long it would be until either, or both, of them came. She pushed her face into Shontay's long, smooth neck, kissing and sucking it hungrily, nibbling the lobe of her ear.

"I want to lick your pussy," she whispered hotly, breathing into Shontay's ear while gently pushing her onto her back. "I want your beautiful pussy . . . let me have your beautiful pussy . . . please . . . please, Shontay."

"Oh Laura . . ."

By now Laura had slipped down to her wonderful little breasts, so perfectly round and firm, and was licking her thick caramel nipples, feeling them grow taut under her tongue, digging her fingers excitedly into the pretty round balls.

"I want to suck you," she panted, teasing Shontay's stiffening, saliva-wet nipples with the tip of her tongue, bringing hot little mewls of sexual delight from deep in the girl's throat.

"Oh Laura . . . please . . . ohhhh!" Shontay sighed, almost inaudibly.

Now, feeling Shontay yield to her caresses, Laura unleashed the full force of her passion, which she had been holding tightly in check for so long. She sucked one delectable, shiny, wet dark brown nipple into her mouth, trying to be gentle, not wanting to alarm Shontay by the full heat of her need, but unable to hold it all back. She sucked the thick, pulpy bud and pinched Shontay's other nipple with her fingers, sucking harder, until she could hear a reaction, a sharp, clotted intake of breath that told her she was on the right track. Shontay's body also clenched spasmodically, suddenly.

"Unhh!" she half-choked. "Oh . . . yes! Unhh!"

Laura was unrelenting. She switched to Shontay's other nipple, now twirling and pinching the wet, erect one with her fingers, devouring the second one with her mouth, sucking it hard, pinching it too with her lips. It was almost as if Laura, being so surprised and thrilled to find these marvelous little breasts where she expected nothing but a flat expanse of skin stretched over hard bone, was intent on sucking the beauties right down her throat.

But Shontay's reaction was not dismay; instead, having her nipples voraciously sucked by Laura in this way seemed to ignite whatever kindling in her body that was not yet burning. She keened and whimpered, rolling and surging and writhing and squirming wildly now under Laura, totally consumed by sexual needs Laura would never have guessed were there.

"Oh yes . . . oh yes!" she gasped, her eyelids fluttering open to watch as Laura squeezed and mouth-mauled her pretty little breasts, her head falling back to the mattress as Laura began quickly to descend lower, afraid that Shontay might even come before she had a chance to kiss her sweet pussy.

Shontay's body was long. Her legs were amazingly long, but her torso was long too, and Laura wanted to spend days just kissing the smooth, sleek, light-brown stretch of her lovely long stomach, so sleek and firm, her ribs a little more defined than most since she was so skinny, her hip bones protruding more, her belly smooth and deep. But Laura was also in a hurry, and she had to resign herself. Save it for later. I want her pussy, and I can smell it.

Shontay was so aroused that the thick, pungent odors of her excited pussy had begun to reach Laura's nose even as she had her mouth stuffed with the girl's delectable caramel nipples, and now, as she descended, the sweet, heady smells grew even thicker, and more erotic. Slipping between the girl's long, thin thighs, she came face to face with the small, gaping, swollen cleft of Shontay's open cunt.

Shontay had a small one, not long and sinuous like the rest of her body, but a modest little aperture, all runny and inviting with juices, the black inner lips puckered and protruding beyond the home provided by the outer folds, the inside a flaming, glistening magenta hole that beckoned Laura's tongue.

"Oh god, honey, it's so pretty," she murmured, spreading away with her thumbs the fibers of moist pubic hair that would get in the way of her tongue-rape.

"Ohhhnnn!" Shontay moaned, looking down her long body at Laura again.

Laura, peeking up over her black-fringed pubic bone, smiled warmly at her. "Are you going to come?" she whispered in a sultry whisper. "I'll bet I can make you come."

Though completely overpowered by sublimely urgent sexual needs, Shontay managed a frightened nod, like an entrapped deer, as if she had never come close to this feeling before. And of course, maybe she hadn't, Laura thought. Didn't she say she never came except by herself? Then this *is* completely new to her.

For some reason, this excited Laura further. It was like fucking a beautiful virgin, one who had thrown up every resistance she could think of but had been finally overcome by sheer dogged adoration and persistence, and the thrill was indescribable. Her thumbs, having spread away the stray hair, found the little hood at the top of Shontay's oozing pussy and pulled the skin back a little on each side, exposing the tiny nubbin of her clit.

It was really quite small, though proportional to the rest of her lovely small pussy, and Laura extended her tongue, touching the tip of it tenderly against the sensitive bud.

"Ungghhhh!" Shontay suddenly groaned, her head falling back again, and the lower part of her body quivering as unbearably sweet sensations shot through her. "Oh god!"

Laura was now in ninth heaven. "Does that feel good? Ummmm. Does that feel good, honey? How about this?"

Now she began licking Shontay's wet, inflamed pussy slowly and sensually, and since it was so small, it was no trouble for Laura to cover the entire slick, magenta blossom with nearly every stroke of her tongue.

"Unh! Ohnnn! Oh god . . . yes! Laura . . ." Shontay gasped, again holding her head up for a second, as if she could see what Laura was doing to her pussy.

"Oh . . . you are going to come so hard," Laura purred, now massaging the flesh on each side of Shontay's pussy as she licked it, again using her thumbs to pulled back the small hood, now tongue-flicking the tiny nubbin of Shontay's clit repeatedly, hearing the high, semi-hysterical whimpering that fought its way out of Shontay's throat.

Shontay was closer now than ever, but still she did not seem to have reached the point of no return. Laura had to concede that it was true, she probably was not an easy comer. God, I would have come about three times by now, she thought. I couldn't take much more of this.

But Shontay was quivering, moaning, twisting, looking down at Laura between her thighs, then letting her head flop back to the mattress, groaning, now undulating her hips in slow, rhythmic fuck motions. Laura knew she could bring her there, but it was a delicious challenge nonetheless. Thinking maybe a little penetration would help, she slid one long forefinger up into the warm, greasy channel of Shontay's cunt, twisting it and tonguing Shontay's swollen clit at the same time.

This seemed to ring Shontay's chimes, and the sexual tension she was feeling immediately seemed to jump up a notch. Her lovely long body flexed, writhing more violently, and the high-pitched, semi-hysterical moaning that seemed half-strangled in her throat became more desperate.

"Hhnnneeee . . . hnnneeee!" she gurgled, now digging her sharp elbows into the mattress and arching her back, quivering so wildly that her wonderful little breasts jiggled and rolled, making Laura want to mouth-maul them again, even though she was heavily involved in her present task. "Hhhnnnneeeee . . . oh god . . . oh god!" Shontay gasped, churning desperately.

"Oh baby . . . oh baby!" Laura purred back to her, redoubling her loving passion.

You *are* going to come, you *are*. I'm going to make you come, I know I can do it.

But Shontay seemed to have reached the breaking point. Her body was so tense, so raw and knotted with unreleased sexual frenzy, that she was shaking uncontrollably, cawing and gurgling in the grip of a frantic desperation, hungering so urgently for an orgasm that tears were actually leaking from the corners of her eyes as she thrashed and clenched and squirmed, trying to come. Then, with shocking suddenness, she collapsed, completely limp, slumping back to the mattress.

"Oh god . . . I can't!" she cried out softly, a wail more than a cry.

Laura looked up and saw that Shontay's face was now slick with tears. Overcome by concern and tenderness, she immediately slid up, enfolding her in her arms, kissing her fervently, warmly, fondling her delicious little breasts with her hands, cooing to her reassuringly.

"Oh, you can . . . you can," she murmured, kissing the tears from Shontay's shiny cheeks, kissing her eyelids. "You can . . . but you're trying too hard."

Shontay gave her a wan, bleak smile, blinking, her eyelashes bejeweled with tears.

Laura kissed her incredibly long neck again, nibbling her earlobe, breathing hotly into her ear. "Didn't it feel good?"

"Oh . . . god yes," Shontay gasped in a vulnerable, faraway voice. "It was . . . heaven."

Laura kissed her lips, a long, lingering kiss that rose in a simmering crescendo to a very fevered pitch. At first Shontay was again reluctant to open her mouth, but soon she was coiling tongues and writhing under Laura as heatedly as before.

"Now you just relax and leave everything to Laura," Laura purred to her. "Just don't try . . . just let it happen, okay?"

With a fetching sniffle, Shontay nodded. Laura slid down her long, smooth, light brown body again and resumed her attentions to Shontay's pretty little pussy, now puffy and glimmering with juices, all soupy and tangy to the taste. Again she slid her finger into it, feeling Shontay jump slightly, hearing a tight, excited gasp. Now, when Laura's tongue began to stroke her clit, Shontay began to moan in a distant, rhapsodic way, as if she were being transported into a realm of the senses she had always feared and desired but never experienced before.

Her moans were soft, but as Laura gradually accelerated the tempo, they became transformed into keening groans and deep, guttural whimpers. Laura knew she was on the right road this time. Oh yes, you're going to do it now, honey. You're going to surprise yourself. Come on . . . come on, just a little farther . . . a little more.

Laura realized, as she had moments ago acknowledged to herself, that she too was about to come. She had never had the kind of difficulty Shontay was having, and by now she could feel the overflow of juice in her crotch. Her pussy was throbbing like a fire alarm. Almost instinctively, she reached down to stroke it with her hand, wanting to get her own body into rhythm with Shontay's, since she knew the girl was about to come. Shontay's orgasm would be enough to trigger her own, she knew.

"Ohhnnnnn! Ohnnnnn god! Oh . . . Jesus!" Shontay moaned, twisting, raising her own hands to her swirling, naked breasts for the first time, pulling her nipples, now churning her pelvis in constant, even circles into Laura's face, clearly more wildly aroused than she had been even moments ago, when she had approached the pinnacle and then turned back.

"Mmmm," Laura hummed happily, massaging her own throbbing clit, now sucking Shontay's cleverly in persistent, rhythmic sucks, bringing the girl to the absolute inescapable brink.

"Oh . . . Laura, I think—" she suddenly gasped. "Oh! Oh, yes!"

Laura's hand moved faster in her own groin. "Yes! Yes, honey! Go for it! Unhhh! Oh god . . . me too!"

"Anngghhh! Ohngg! Unh! Unh!" Shontay began panting frantically, her moans now constricted into tight, hysterical little squeaks as she was sucked up into an inevitable crushing finish.

Laura, in the back of her brain cursing her bad timing, actually began to come before Shontay did. She could feel the molten honeyfire begin flooding her body, feel her muscles contracting and her toes curling, feel the birth of a throbbing star deep inside her belly followed by wrenching spasms as she began to be swallowed by it. Shontay, on the other hand, clenched, and clenched, her long, sleek body straining, her knees twitching up and to the sides spastically, her face seized by a terrible, agonizing rapture, and suddenly dissolved into a shuddering, mewling wreck as a huge, inundating orgasm engulfed her.

At first she made no sound but a raw, choked cawing in her throat. Then a low, keening moan seemed to travel up from deep in her body to her mouth.

"Unnhhhhoowwwnnooaauunnggghhhhh!" she moaned, starting softly but then erupting in a loud cry that reminded Laura of how cats sounded when they were doing it.

Once this cry was out, a flood of wild squeals and groans escaped from her lips as her body began to thrash and quiver with each successive wave of her orgasm.

"Unhh! Auungghhhh! Oh . . . oh yes! Mmmnngggeeeee! Auuggnnhhh!" she groaned, coming in fierce bursts, her body almost shattered by each sharp, rupturing spasm.

Laura, though her own orgasm had not approached this intensity, was still half-crippled from the sweet spasms that were only now beginning to subside in her body. She slid up to embrace Shontay, feeling the heat that both of them were generating as it wound around their two naked bodies like a hot sheet, linking them together in a warm, throbbing union of sweet coming that took another thirty seconds or so to finally fade. Even then, Shontay was thrilled by four or five aftershocks that seemed to paralyze her as she stared dreamily into Laura's eyes.

"Unhhh! Oh god . . . there's another one!" she gasped, burrowing her face into Laura's shoulder and shuddering until it passed.

Laura simply held her, without speaking, stroking her long, smooth, naked back with her fingertips as Shontay suffered through the excruciating delights of this stupendous climax. They clung together for about five minutes. When it was over, Laura noticed that Shontay's cheeks were still damp, and she daubed them dry with the edge of the sheet.

"I guess that wasn't anything to cry over, was it," she murmured with a warm grin.

Shontay smiled back, suddenly bashful, so charming in a woman who often seemed like an ice sculpture. She shook her head. "I . . . never . . ."

But she couldn't get it out.

Laura kissed her mouth. "I know you never. Now you have."

"What about you?"

"I did it the way we first planned. You were too . . . busy to hear me groaning and gasping, that's all."

Shontay's brow knitted up. Her pale brown eyes, so electric moments ago, but now clear glowing pools, showed her deep concern. "But that's not right. I mean, you got me there. Boy, did you ever get me there." She made a funny face. "I don't think I've ever been there before." She paused, still scrutinizing Laura's face with concern, as if Laura were somehow still bottled up and ready to pop. "It's really not fair for me not to help you get there too."

Laura smiled wryly. "I'd sure like to go where you went. Looked like it felt good."

Shontay smiled, embarrassed. "You watched me. I feel kind of shy now."

"No need. You were beautiful."

Shontay's brow was still knitted. Without another word, she slid down Laura's body, pushing apart Laura's thighs with both hands. She remained silent, but Laura could almost feel her stare, even though she couldn't see her face.

"Laura . . . I didn't know what you meant when you said that about mine . . . but yours is really . . . lovely too. I didn't know it would be so pretty . . . so curvy and pink. It's like a seashell."

"Unhh!" Laura gasped, feeling a hot arrow of pleasure shoot through her whole body as Shontay's tongue first touched her pussy.

"Oh . . . I didn't do it wrong, did I?"

"You're doing it . . . just perfectly," Laura panted, falling back, parting her thighs further. "Yes. Oh yes! Unhhh!"

About a minute passed while Shontay patiently explored Laura's tingling wet pussy with her tongue, going at it tentatively but not shyly, determined to reward Laura for the stunning experience she herself had just had. She was unsmiling, very serious, as her face appeared for a moment above Laura's pubic mound.

"I even like the taste," she said, grinning suddenly, delightedly.

Then her head dropped again, and Laura moaned as the sensations grew more and more urgent. Her first orgasm had merely been a byproduct of Shontay's thrilling seizure, a little like yawning when you saw someone else doing it, but this time Laura gave it her full attention. And though Shontay was not very experienced, she was very ardent and deliberate. In about a minute, Laura was groaning and shuddering through a sweet and powerful climax that made her first one seem like an accidental sneeze.

Shontay patiently waited for Laura to recover her senses, which took a few minutes, before smiling and looking self-satisfied. "You do it pretty easily," she said softly, seriously. "Wish I could do that."

Laura had finally regained her breath. She put a finger on Shontay's wonderful, sensual lips. "It only takes a little practice."

She didn't know if she might not be lying, though. Some women might never climax with ease. It might always be a little harder for Shontay than for her.

At this moment, Willie leapt up onto the bed and quickly jumped between them. He looked half-astonished, it seemed, at both of them, then began to purr loudly. Laura and Shontay laughed and began to pet him.

"Hello, Willie," Shontay said, scratching him behind the ears. "Don't you wish you could do what we just did? Laura just did something to me nobody else ever did."

Willie licked Shontay's long brown arm.

Laura winked at her. "I think Willie better watch his step. I'm getting jealous."

Shontay looked askance at Laura, half-embarrassed again. She knew what Laura was talking about. Their relationship was irreversibly altered now. No going back. They had fucked, heatedly. They would doubtless do it again, and again, in coming days and weeks. Where there had been distance and suspicion, there now was intimacy. Oh god, Laura thought, seeing the expression on Shontay's face, which reminded her so much of Lila, of Tamara, of the others who were so afraid of what they had done at this moment.

But instead of dwelling on this thought, Shontay brightened again almost immediately. "Do you think we could . . . do that again?" she asked, almost shyly, looking down at her hand on Willie's fur so she would not have to meet Laura's eyes. Then she quickly looked up. "I mean, after we rest a little, you know. Not right away."

"Mmmmm, what's the matter with right away?" Laura asked, reaching across Willie to caress her face, letting her hand fall to Shontay's naked breasts.

By now Willie was truly in the way, between them, and he seemed to know it. With the instinctive escapist skill of cats, he speedily leaped over Shontay's long legs and bounded off the bed onto the floor. Laura had Shontay's long, warm, naked body clasped hard against hers and her mouth glued heatedly to Shontay's before either of them quite knew what was happening. Shontay responded happily, yielding her mouth, rubbing her body against Laura's, coiling tongues hungrily.

"Only if I can kiss that perfect bottom of yours," Laura whispered to her, letting both hands fall to the wonderful little rump she had admired for months. "I love your little ass. I want your little ass."

"You're going to make me blush, if you don't watch out."

Laura nuzzled her everywhere she could reach with her mouth. "Mmmm, I'm going to make you glow . . . I'm going to make you beg."

Shontay pulled back, almost flirtatiously, batting her eyelashes at Laura, acting faux-coy, twisting her body so that her ass was sticking up, more visible. "You like that bony little thing?"

Now Laura's caresses grew more aggressive. She squeezed one round, spongy-hard little bun with her hand, a delicious, exciting squeeze that made her whole body tingle and made Shontay gasp and instinctively gnaw her lower lip.

"I don't feel any bone there," Laura whispered, eyes flaring. "Just wonderful ass." She slid her fingers into the crack between Shontay's round little buns. "Turn over. Let me kiss that fantastic back of yours too."

With slow, feigned reluctance, Shontay turned onto her stomach, stretching out luxuriously next to Laura, extending the full length of her smooth, supple, slender body, relishing the feeling of Laura's eyes roaming excitedly all over it.

"You are so beautiful . . . how can you hide all this beautiful flesh under those awful suits you wear?" Laura said in an awed, hushed voice, unable to control her renewed lust.

She didn't realize what she had said, about the suits, until it came out of her mouth, but it turned out that Shontay was more thrilled by Laura's enchantment with her naked body than she was hurt by Laura's criticism of her taste in clothes.

"It isn't beautiful. It's skinny," she said, pouting. "And too tall."

That was all Laura needed to unlock the torrents of fresh desire she was feeling, and she immediately straddled the backs of Shontay's thighs and began giving her a slow, sensual back massage. She had earlier thought she could spend a year just kissing this long, smooth brown back anyway, and now she had the chance. She began at the nape of Shontay's neck, truly making love to it and to Shontay's thin shoulders so hungrily that Shontay began shivering and giggling in a soft, sexy voice.

"What's the matter, you don't like the way I dress?" she tried to tease Laura, but very quickly she was panting and even mewling softly as Laura turned up the heat.

Laura kissed her way slowly down the shallow valley formed by Shontay's spine, then back up again, taking constant detours onto the smooth, resilient flesh of the rest of her back, tickling the sensitive nerves under her shoulder blades, which indeed were more prominent than most due to her thin frame. On her second time down the spinal column, Laura's lips arrived at the upward curve of Shontay's sacrum, highlighted on either side by a delicious deep dimple. Oh god, it's perfection! Laura thought, kissing one dimple with carefully controlled but burning adoration, then the other.

Shontay squirmed and whimpered. "God, Laura . . . you're getting me all hot and sticky again. So quick."

Laura's hand dipped between her thin, sleek thighs, finding the small, wet blossom of Shontay's cunt again, while she kissed her way from the second dimple over to the firm, swelling moons of Shontay's small, jutting ass. It was a compact ass, small but beautifully shaped, and she spent the next minutes worshipping it thoroughly with her mouth and her fingers, kneading and squeezing the hard little melons, kissing them, then biting them suggestively, even snarling softly with hungry passion, until Shontay was squirming and whimpering, looking back over her shoulder, grimacing in pleasure, as if fascinated by the sensations Laura was arousing in her perfect little bottom.

Laura's attentions were making Shontay a lot wetter, too. Laura could feel the warm, buttery fluids bathing her fingers as she lightly massaged Shontay's small pussy, reluctant to do it too fast since she didn't want Shontay to come again before she had finished her selfish little feast. By now she knew that Shontay was unlikely to go off unexpectedly, but still she didn't want to risk it. I want to drive her wild, she realized. I want her to claw the sheets and scream. There's only us, nobody can hear us, no Kendra, no Gibsons, except this long, lovely one. Shontay . . . I want you to scream.

"Ohhnnnn!" Shontay moaned, again looking back at Laura, her face contorted in an expression of fierce sexual arousal. "Unhhhhh! Oh *god*, that feels good!"

It's going to feel a lot better than that, darling, Laura thought, beginning to part Shontay's tight little ass cheeks with her fingers and to run the tip of her tongue into the dark, warm crack between them. At first Shontay seemed not to notice, but as Laura's tongue descended further into her crack, she could not help but notice. Her hips shimmied in a sharp, excited spasm, and she tried to twist her body to the side, but Laura was strong and held her steady.

"What . . . are you doing?" Shontay whimpered.

"Mmmm, I'm loving your ass like nobody's ever loved it before," Laura purred.

"Jesus . . . that's what I'm afraid of," Shontay gasped, with a repressed giggle.

"Doesn't it feel good?"

"It feels wonderful!"

The tip of her tongue had finally arrived at Shontay's tight little black rosebud, her ultimate destination, but she already knew it would be too shocking to the girl simply to enter it without warning. Her fingers in Shontay's pussy were all gooey now with warm nectars, and as she slid one up higher into Shontay's crack, she moved her mouth to the side and took a sizable piece of ass-flesh into it, biting it gingerly but firmly.

"Anngghh!" Shontay yelped, distracted enough by the momentary squirt of pleasurable pain not to notice Laura's forefinger sliding up into her anus.

Now Laura peppered the smooth, brown moons with love bites, repeating her first bite everywhere, sucking chunks of firm flesh into her mouth, clamping her teeth on them, burrowing her finger deeper into Shontay's ass at the same time. Shontay mewled and squirmed, but after a few seconds she seemed to know something unusual had happened.

"Oh!" she gasped. "What's that? Unghhhh! Oh . . . Laura," she moaned, her eyes full of hot sex and unanswerable questions as they caught Laura's.

Shontay appeared so shocked that she could not understand where Laura was going with this, but Laura knew very well. Now that she had somewhat loosened the opening, the true rape she had planned was possible.

"Oh, sorry," she winked at Shontay, teasing her, but letting her eyes smoke with sexual threats at the same time.

She extracted her finger from the girl's back track, dropping her hand again to Shontay's dripping pussy. Now she returned her tongue to the wonderfully deep little crack between Shontay's smooth brown buns and, using her free hand to pull them apart, slid the tip of it into the girl's rectum, wriggling it in quickly and as deep as it would go.

"Ahhnnnnneeeee!" Shontay suddenly screamed, though to Laura's ears it was only a hint of the screams she hoped were coming. "Ohhhnnn . . . shit!"

But by now Laura had her in the grip of a thrilling, magnetic sexual rhythm that would not let her go. Now Laura increased the speed of the two fingers she was using to rub Shontay's flowing, throbbing slit, swirling her taut little clit in a hot frenzy now, and driving her tongue deep into the girl's ass. Shontay whooped and clenched her firm little ass cheeks and squirmed, but Laura was aware that she really didn't want to get away, even though the sensations were very intense.

"Oh god . . . what are you doing! God, Laura . . . stop!"

Laura wasn't exactly in a position to discuss it, and in answer she withdrew her tongue temporarily from Shontay's pretty little asshole and began biting her round, swelling, hard buns again, rubbing her pussy even harder and faster.

"Mmmnnggeee!" Shontay squealed, now perceptibly jumping up a notch in tension, so that Laura now knew the girl would come any time. "Oh! Ohnggg!"

"I'm making you come," Laura panted, sinking herself into a passionate depravity that she could barely control. Shontay's long, smooth brown body, though slim, was wildly desirable, especially in this writhing, flexing, quivering state as Shontay approached another orgasm.

"Oh god . . . you're right!" Shontay gasped, dropping her head back to the mattress, even lifting her ass a little to give Laura easier access, swirling it back and up slowly into Laura's face. "Oh god Laura . . . yes! Ungghh! Yes!"

It was a beautiful ass, and Laura worshipped and passion-mauled it at the same time, biting and excitedly pinching the smooth brown moons, now pulling her hand up from Shontay's dripping pussy for a moment to pry both of her buns apart and stab her tongue deep into Shontay's tight little rectum.

"Unggghhh! Oh! Mmmnnggggeee . . . oh . . . Laura! Oh . . . I'm going to—"

Shontay's long, thin body grew suddenly stiff. Laura, her tongue wriggling deep in the girl's moist, clenching asshole, knew she was going to come. Nothing could stop it. Dropping her hand again to

Shontay's streaming pussy, she found Shontay's clit with two fingers and pressed it hard, then rubbed it vigorously, tongue-fucking her ass in a fierce frenzy at the same time.

Shontay's stiffened body suddenly jackknifed up off the bed, a violent, twisting, surging motion that almost dislodged Laura's face from its happy haven between the girl's taut little buns.

"AUUNNGGGGHHNNIIIEEEEEE!" she screamed, collapsing into a mass of shuddering spasms that Laura sustained by continuing to tongue-fuck her ass and rub her pussy. "OHHNNGG! Ungghhhh! Oh . . . shit! Oh Laura . . . auungghhhhh! Nnnggmmmiieeee!"

Her climax seemed about three times more intense than the first one, and about three times longer too. She wailed and screamed and writhed as Laura refused to let her stop, coming, then slumping and panting, then coming again, two full orgasms punctuated by a whole sequence of smaller shocks, until finally she lay gasping and moaning on her stomach, wincing as the last aftershock made her wince and shiver.

Slowly, Laura removed her fingers from Shontay's pussy and her tongue from the girl's pretty little asshole, which she had tongue-raped enthusiastically. Shontay was still trying to regain her breath and her senses. Laura kissed her way up the girl's naked back, now much more tenderly, again brushing away the hair from her neck and kissing the nape sensually.

Shontay stirred and smiled. "You don't give up, do you," she murmured, hoarsely. "I never knew anybody like you."

"Mmmm, I don't know how anybody who could come like that could give up sex," Laura whispered in her ear.

"Are you kidding?" Shontay grinned, rolling over now, facing Laura. "I never came like that in my life. If I had, I probably wouldn't have given it up."

Laura tried to kiss her, but Shontay playfully turned her face away.

"Would you mind rinsing out your mouth before doing that?" she asked. "I love to kiss you, but you just had your tongue in my . . . you know where."

Laura grinned. "Honey, it's clean as a whistle. I just cleaned it out."

"You sure did," Shontay grinned back. She was suddenly gripped by a quick, intense shiver. "See, it makes me almost come again just thinking of it. But do it anyway, okay? Just to make me feel better?"

Making a face, Laura hopped off the bed and went to the bathroom, rinsing out her mouth and returning in seconds.

"I came back for my kiss. It's the least you can give me after coming twice."

Shontay looked very sultry as she welcomed Laura into her arms. "I bet you can too," she purred sexily, much more seductive than Laura had ever dreamed possible. "Twice, I mean. Why don't you stay here tonight? I think I'd be lonely now if you went downstairs. Just stay here, sleep with me, and you can go down and dress before work."

Laura kissed her. "We might not get much sleep."

Shontay looked demurely down, shy and at the same time very excited by what had transpired. "We've got all the rest of our lives to sleep, right?"

***

Laura drifted awake in the morning to the sweet, faintly erotic odors of Shontay's naked flesh pressed against her cheek. It happened to be one of the girl's exquisite, teacup breasts, so round and firm, the nipple so soft and delectable that she could not keep from taking it into her mouth. Shontay stirred and moaned, coming awake. She watched Laura languorously sucking her nipple.

"I never slept with anybody before," she said quietly, stroking the hair away from Laura's forehead. "Like this, I mean." Laura looked at her quizzically, holding Shontay's wet, caramel-colored nipple in her lips. "I always made them go home. Oh, that feels good."

"Mmmm, are you going to make *me* go home?"

Shontay's eyes sparkled with happiness. "You only did it to me about four or five times last night. Don't you ever get tired?"

"Not of 'doing it' to *you*. Do you get tired?"

Shontay shook her head, and they were quickly into another round, making love as if the world outside them no longer existed. At work, Laura was relieved that their duties and responsibilities were entirely separate, and that there was no opportunity for them to meet and betray their sudden intimacy. For the next week, while Shontay's parents were still away, they met each evening for dinner in one or the other apartment, and spent the rest of the night in delicious fucking.

Then she and Shontay had a tender parting on the night before Shontay's parents were due to return. It happened that Laura was scheduled for a conference in Tucson the next day, and they would be apart for the first time in a week.

"Tucson?" Shontay whined.

"Are you going to miss me?"

A big tear was already forming at the bottom of one of Shontay's pale brown eyes. But she sniffled, then wiped it away, all the cold reserve returning to her face.

"Of course not," she said, glaring at Laura. "Why should I miss you?"

"Because nobody can make you come the way I can?" Laura teased.

"Maybe I'll find somebody," Shontay said, with a toss of the head. "Some guys like tall skinny girls."

"Some women like them too," Laura said. "Me, for one."

Now Shontay became pliant, fawn-like. "Will you miss *me*?"

"I'll call you every night."

Why am I saying these things? Laura wondered. She adored Shontay, but she knew she didn't feel the kind of desperate, burning, scorching, searing lust for her that she felt for, say, Deshona. Still, she and Shontay working together had brought Shontay along to a new place, a sexual oasis where she could enjoy a sweet and blissfully intense pleasure that was only possible with Laura. It was hard not to be touched by it, even moved, and Laura gave in without a fight.

"Here's my number," Shontay said, scribbling on the back of her business card. "Don't call me at work. Too dangerous. In fact, we should probably just keep pretending we don't know each other."

What a good idea! Laura thought. Why couldn't I have done that with Randi? Yvette? All the others?

She had actually grown quite fond of Shontay during this week, somehow warmed by Shontay's carefully-masked vulnerability, and her fresh sense of wonder at the sex they shared. No longer was she the cold, calculating, remote bitch Laura had initially thought her to be, the careerist, the haughty tall girl who looked down both physically and socially on everyone. She was instead a delightful young girl who was having several orgasms each day because Laura was wildly infatuated with her as a bed partner.

On the flight to Tucson, Laura even felt pangs of separation from her and was very troubled. Her life was complicated enough, she thought, and screwing her neighbors' daughter could only make it worse. For example, could she and Shontay make love in her, Laura's, apartment when Shontay's parents might be home upstairs? It had been bad enough trying to muffle every stray groan and gasp before with her visitors; what would it be like if Shontay were about to scream in ecstasy? (And Laura had learned how to make her scream, and also whinny uncontrollably.)

The conference was dull but enlivened by Laura unexpectedly running into Lila, and the rest was history. It took a little persuading, as it usually did with the profoundly inhibited Lila, but Laura quickly got her into bed again, and they spent the rest of their few hours at the conference screwing heatedly. Laura forgot to call Shontay, as she had promised she would. She had forgotten about Shontay entirely, and Shontay was not pleased.

On the phone, when Laura finally did get around to calling, she was distant, haughty, querulous, cold by turns, everything Laura had found her to be before their warming—their thrilling, sensitive, and multi-orgasmic nights together in bed in her parents' apartment.

"You said you would call!" she whined at Laura.

"I . . . couldn't," Laura said, truthfully. "I was too tired. The damn dinner went on forever. I'm sorry. I was thinking of you." Liar.

Shontay punished her a few more minutes before softening. Laura had called her at home right after rushing from Lila's room over to her own to change. Her body was still tingling from fucking with Lila only moments earlier. She felt guiltier than ever about lying to Shontay, but there was no choice.

"You'll never guess what I did," Shontay said, softly. "Last night. I was thinking of you at that conference . . . and I did . . . you know, what we did together. The first time. You know . . . by myself. But I was thinking of you. It was the best ever, that way. I miss you, Laura."

Laura was touched, and troubled, at the same time. "I miss you too, darling," she whispered.

"Call me tonight? I could do it while I'm talking to you on the phone. I'll bet that would be fun."

"I promise."

It wasn't easy, but that night she had told Lila she had a mild headache and needed a quick nap. She went to her room, promising to meet Lila in about an hour, and phoned Shontay, who was eagerly awaiting her call. Then, in one of the most exciting phone conversations Laura had experienced in recent years, Shontay brought herself to two orgasms while Laura listened and murmured to her.

She also begged to know that Laura was doing it too, at the same time. Wanting to save herself for Lila later, Laura had complied by moaning and faking it, pretending to come when Shontay's voice on the other end was out of control, gasping and squeaking a little, then sighing, feeling mortified and massively guilty for this deception. Why couldn't I just go ahead and do it? she had wondered.

But Shontay was none the wiser, and their conversation concluded with lengthy very soft murmurings of affection that Laura figured would hold the darling, complex girl for a few days until she got back.

**

She came awake a few days later Laura in Shontay's bed—in Shontay's apartment, too, instead of the Gibsons' place above her own—

but dreaming of Lila. It was a real dream, and guilt or chagrin would have to wait until later. In the dream, Laura was on her back, and Lila was on top of her. Both were naked. Laura could feel Lila's very firm breasts and the thick soft bulbs of her nipples moving against her own skin. Lila slithered her long tongue deep into Laura's mouth. Laura almost came in her sleep, and then slid abruptly into consciousness.

She was face to face with Shontay, who was still in a deep sleep, breathing evenly, looking pure and lovely. When awake, Shontay's face had an habitually cold and arrogant cast, which she had now partially softened due to her fondness for Laura, when they were together. But in sleep she looked as angelic as a child. Her hair, usually pulled back severely, came down for fucking with Laura, and now it was tangled and drooping across her face in stray locks, making her look very sensual and fetching.

They had fucked at first in an insatiable frenzy, spurred on by the memory of Shontay masturbating while Laura listened on the telephone from Tucson. Then they had settled into a more relaxed rhythm, though by midnight both were so exhausted they could barely move. Laura understood why Shontay was zonked. On the other hand, she wondered how she could possibly be so oversexed as to have dreams of fucking with Lila after what she and Shontay had done before falling asleep.

Over Shontay's thin, light brown shoulder she could see the clock on her vanity table. It was six-ten a.m. She had to go to work—so did Shontay, for that matter—and had had no intention of spending the night. Now she would have to drive home, shower, change, and rush to make it on time.

She kissed Shontay's cheek. "Good morning, sunshine," she whispered. "I've got to go home and change for work."

Shontay smiled drowsily, stretching, slowly coming awake. In fact, she could not stop smiling as she gazed into Laura's eyes.

"Did we really do what I think we did last night?" she asked softly.

Laura nodded, kissing her mouth. "I guess it was worth waiting for, right?"

Shontay frowned slightly. "Are you sure I satisfy you? I mean, I can tell you must've had a lot of . . . other girls. It makes me a little . . . jealous . . . and also a little insecure."

Laura gulped. How could she just get up and leave with Shontay feeling like that? Instead, she embraced her, kissed her, rubbed her whole body against Shontay's long, skinny body in a way that made them both remember the previous night in acute detail.

"Darling, you do more than satisfy me," she purred. "You make me shimmer and glow. When I'm away from you, I just dream of the way your lips feel on my pussy."

"Really?" Shontay's high forehead knitted up.

"Really." She brushed the hair away from Shontay's smooth cheek, touched by the girl's innocence. "Do you think of me?"

"All the time. I think mostly of when we did it the first time. I was so scared. You wouldn't believe how scared I was. I give a good imitation of courage, but I'm really scared shitless most of the time."

Laura squeezed her tightly and nibbled her earlobe. "Welcome to the club," she breathed softly into Shontay's ear. "You know . . . I have to go home and change, but I can't seem to make myself let this beautiful body go."

"You mean this skinny, bony, gangly body?"

Now Laura was kissing her the way she had kissed her last night. "I mean this long . . . beautiful . . . slender body," she murmured, kissing

Shontay's upper chest and collarbones and throat, now kneading the girl's charming teacup breasts with her fingers. "I think I suddenly need another one before we stop."

"Oh god, me too! Unhhhhh! Oh . . . Laura . . . yes, I think we have just a little time. Do that again. Please!"

While kissing her throat and her delectably straight collarbones, and fondling her small breasts, Laura had dropped one hand between their bodies and lightly pinched Shontay's small clit, very gently, only enough to give her a happy twinge, but apparently enough to make her blood leap.

Sometimes in the morning, awakening after a night of exhausting sex, Laura felt a surprisingly fresh and insistent flash of lust. Both of them seemed to feel it at this instant, and they kissed hungrily, panting and whimpering.

"Touch me . . . touch me too," Laura panted to Shontay.

Shontay dropped her hand. "Like this?"

"Yes! Oh . . . yes! Unhhh!"

Shontay's pale brown eyes were wide and shiny, locked with Laura's, throbbing. "Oh!" she gasped. Her eyes rolled up.

"Yes . . . yes darling yes oh . . . god yes!"

For the next several seconds they kissed with extra sensuality, intermingling their tongues and their moist breath, their naked breasts brushing and their fingers moving rapidly below, their lower bodies beginning to pitch and roll in unison. The moment approached. They were tightly synchronized, looking into each other's eyes, moaning softly.

"Come with me, baby," Laura panted. "I'm going to . . ."

"Oh Laura . . . oh Laura yes . . . oh Laura! Unhhh! Oh . . . Laura! Oh!"

Shontay's eyes rolled up again, and she began to come. Laura was conscious for only the split second it took her to see this, and then she began to come too, an exquisite, hard, piercing ecstasy that felt almost painful in its intensity, the final one in a long string of orgasms that had started the night before. Her body clenched so hard that it was almost like a charley-horse, and recovering from it left her dazed and speechless.

She could tell by gazing at Shontay's face that Shontay's orgasm had been equally sharp. After the grimace of near-pain faded from her features, Shontay was still stunned and numb.

"Excuse me," she half-coughed, clearing her throat, after a minute or so had elapsed. "That really . . . sort of got to me. It almost hurt, it was so hard."

"Tell me about it," Laura whispered in acknowledgement, tightening her embrace. "For a minute I was paralyzed." She laughed softly and kissed Shontay's gleaming wide forehead, now shiny with a thin film of sweat. "I guess you don't have to worry any more about satisfying me."

Shontay glowed with half-embarrassed pride.

Now that they had patched up things and improved Shontay's confidence, Laura felt more relaxed about hurrying home to dress for work. Coming into her building, she actually ran into Mr. Gibson, Shontay's father, coming down to the lobby to get his morning paper. They exchanged morning pleasantries, but Laura could not ignore the look in his eyes. He clearly thought it very odd, and a little scandalous, that she would be coming in at seven o'clock in the morning, still dressed in yesterday's work clothes, looking a little frazzled and worn. Laura remembered how she and Dawn had nearly raised the roof with their cries and fierce, ecstatic shrieks only a few nights ago; she still had no idea whether the Gibsons had been home to overhear them.

This thought made her blush pretty deeply. Oh, forget it, she told herself. It's none of his business what I do. I'm just a little sleepy and dreamy and tingling all over, she smiled. After a night (and a brief awakening) full of thrilling sex. And with your own daughter, too, Mr. Respectable Gibson. Did you know she likes to suck my pretty pussy? Wouldn't that put frost on your balls?

***

Ever since Laura and Taneesha had run into Shontay in the hallway outside Laura's apartment—a scene so painful to remember that Laura avoided anything but a high-level awareness in her mind that it had indeed happened—Laura had been tormented by her realization that Shontay's feelings for her were somehow deeper than she had known. She kicked herself for not having understood it.

Though at work Shontay was aloof, cold, implacable, and apparently much disliked by her direct reports, with Laura she was soft, vulnerable, pliant, and warm, full of delight in her own body, which before Laura she had apparently come to hate and detest for its long, bony frame and sharp angles, and also her inability to come very easily. Before Laura, she confessed, she had never climaxed with another person—meaning a man, of course—only by masturbating.

Laura had quickly put an end to that, and with her Shontay now had several orgasms each time, some of them stupendous shockers that left her weak and gasping. For Shontay, Laura realized belatedly, it was like being reborn. She had blossomed, at least when she was with Laura. She was relaxed, funny, sensual, and very affectionate. She had even left her old baggy business suits in the closet and began to show off a more stylish wardrobe at work—which Laura, fearing a scene, had only detected by spying around corners—one that more successfully flattered her long, slender legs and charming little rump.

Laura cursed herself for not having seen these signs. Anyone would have noticed them. You might not want to call it 'love,' but it was surely a deep sexual attachment and also a deep affection they shared. For all Laura knew, Shontay did think of it as 'love'. She certainly had seemed startled and pained to see Laura with another woman (or girl, Laura thought; it was hard to think of the delicious 'Valley Girl' Taneesha as a woman, though she fucked like one). Shontay, seeing them, had clearly been devastated. Laura could still see the big, silvery tears sliding silently down her smooth, light brown cheeks, her magical pale brown eyes above them stricken and lost.

For nearly two weeks now at work Laura had played cat-and-mouse, trying to avoid her, coming early, leaving late, skirting the areas where Shontay was certain to be. She wondered if Shontay might not be doing the same thing, since they never ran into one another. But the guilt kept gnawing at her, and then the desire, for she actually missed Shontay. Their intimacy had been unexpected, but Laura found that it was captivating. And the more she recalled Shontay standing in the hallway with tears sliding down her cheeks, the more she felt a deep urge to comfort her, to enfold her, to reassure her (by what, more lies? she wondered), and ultimately to take off her pretty new clothes and rub against her until Shontay exploded in ecstasies even more intense than the ones she had experienced so far.

Laura did not know how to deal with this impasse. Shontay could be frighteningly cold and withering in her personal manner, and Laura realized she was a little afraid of her (probably the reason Shontay's employees feared her, too). She could be cutting. She could be an ice pillar of scorn. And Laura knew she herself deserved whatever was coming her way, which made it harder to invite it.

Trying to turn her thoughts to other things, she contemplated moving to a new place. She had lied about it to Taneesha, but the very process of lying had made her wonder if it might not be a good idea. Maybe it was just a peculiar architectural flaw that made the sounds generated in her apartment so audible in the one above. She never experienced such anxieties at Sara's place, or Deshona's, or

Bonnie's. And god knows, we sure whoop it up sometimes, she thought. It's only in my place that I feel this terrible fear that they're going to hear us shrieking.

She was thinking of this so hard one evening as she came home from work that she barely noticed the Gibsons wheeling their stylish and expensive luggage out the door to their Mercedes as she was checking for her mail. They smiled at her vaguely, and she returned the abstracted, neighborly smile they had all apparently agreed on. Then, as she was looking through her mail before heading for the elevator, it occurred to her that they were leaving . . . for a vacation, or a meeting, or something.

Oh god, does that mean Shontay will be coming back over here to feed the cat? she wondered.

As far as she knew, no one showed up the first night, which was the actual night the Gibsons had left. At least, Laura heard no sounds overhead. Though she usually heard little from them when they were home, occasionally a floorboard would creak, or there would be a distant thump, as if something were dropped. She heard nothing.

This made her all the more nervous on the second evening, because if Shontay were dropping by to feed Willie, she certainly would not wait much longer. And in fact, Laura did hear a noise upstairs on the second evening, a definite creak. She's there! she thought.

Laura took a deep breath. I'm going up there. I'm going to knock on the door. I'm going to . . . what? I'm going to apologize. I'm going to tell her that I wouldn't have hurt her for the world. I'm going to tell her I'm just so sorry . . .

She clenched her fists and gritted her teeth, pacing, all in the effort to get courage, to be honest and forthright, to face up to whatever pain she had caused and try to remedy the situation. Seconds later, before she could think of it anymore and allow herself to back out, she was heading up the stairs next to the elevator. She reached the ninth floor and marched resolutely down to the Gibsons' door and knocked.

Then, as she stood waiting, all her courage suddenly left her, draining away like the water in the bottom of a basin. It quickly dawned on her that Shontay would not open the door since she would know it could only be one of two unpleasant possibilities: either a rapist or burglar had got into the building, or it was Laura.

Her heart almost stopped when she heard a small click inside, behind the door. Then she realized it was the tiny hatch-door on the little peep hole in the middle of the door, about average eye-height. She had one on her own peep hole, since it was the same door. Everything was the same. Why couldn't they just make a stupid hole and leave the little hatch-door off? she wondered, knowing that Shontay—or someone, at least—was inside inspecting her now, looking at her, deciding whether to open the door.

"Shontay . . . it's me," Laura burst out, not having prepared to say anything, just hearing the words rush from her mouth in a hushed but semi-hysterical flood.

Still, nothing. No movement or sound from behind the door. Laura looked directly at the peep hole, composing her face into a soft, smiling, friendly mode. Just dropped by to say hi, her face tried to say. I'm . . . oh, you know, just friendly, neighborly Laura, not trying to . . . force myself on you or anything. Just wanted to talk, that's all. She smiled, then was afraid she had smiled too broadly, too falsely, and so shrunk her smiling muscles a little to appear more formal, more restrained.

Whether this strategy worked, or whether Shontay too found the moment becoming unbearable, the door was unlocked and slowly it opened—just a crack, though. Shontay peered out at Laura, her face expressionless.

"Hello . . . Laura," she said, very softly. Her eyes were intense and unrelenting, holding Laura's, boring into Laura's. "What do you want?"

The silence in the hallway where Laura was standing was painful, like a mausoleum, the place where dead dreams went to repose. Laura twisted her fingers.

"I wanted . . . to talk to you."

"That's all?"

Laura nodded.

"Talk, then."

Laura thought of asking to be invited in, then thought better of it. "I . . . wanted to . . . explain."

"You ain't got nothing to explain to me, girl," Shontay snapped, without, however, raising her voice. Her pale, fantastic, light brown eyes glowed with fierce hostility.

Laura had never heard her lapse into this kind of dialect before, which gave added emphasis to Shontay's controlled fury. No wonder I was afraid of her, Laura thought. Look at how stiff she is . . . and god, she looks magnificent when she's angry, with her regal, fierce contempt, her nostrils twitching like that. Laura fought against the clear realization that it was sexually arousing.

She shrugged, not disguising her feeling of defeat. "I wanted to apologize," she said, softly.

She let her eyes do the pleading, hoping to see some sign of softening in this magnificent, haughty, regal creature whose eyes burned and whose chin was held higher than normal, at an imperious height, which made Laura feel even smaller. Shontay glowered at her.

"Go ahead," she breathed finally, almost inaudibly, as if trying to decide whether to be bored or even angrier. "Apologize."

"Look . . . it's kind of hard to do it just . . . standing here. Could I come in? I won't stay but a minute."

Shontay glowered at her. She pushed the door open further and stepped back. Laura, very tentatively, as if she were going to be sliced and shredded instantly by invisible knives, stepped inside. Nervously glancing around Shontay's tall, angular body, she saw Willie, the cat, in the living room, a blur of white fluff with iridescent turquoise eyes, looking at them both. She brought her eyes—reluctantly, fearing the fiery anger there—back to Shontay's.

But now she saw in them what she had not been able to detect in the dim hallway: the faint, insistent throbbing of a deep and real pain, though it was almost successfully masked by the hideous and threatening anger Laura had initially responded to. But seeing it was, curiously, a relief to her. At least she's human, Laura thought, watching Shontay close the door. She did not fasten the deadbolt lock, clearly expecting a short visit, and also making it clear, in case Laura should be devious enough to have any ideas of reconciliation, that nothing more than stammered apologies would be tolerated.

Shontay did not move. She did not try to draw Laura further into the apartment.

"Go ahead."

"Shontay . . . that girl you saw me with is . . . the niece of a friend of mine, a business associate, actually," Laura began, sounding to herself horribly false and treacly.

Shontay looked at her, expressionless again, and said nothing. The silence propelled Laura forward.

"It was just . . . something that happened. I didn't mean to hurt you."

Shontay nodded, a very slight, menacing up and down movement of her head. Her sensual lips were pressed together in a straight line, her eyes hard.

"You didn't," she said in a clipped voice.

"Oh." Laura paused uncomfortably. "I—"

"Is that all?"

"No, it's not 'all'.

Shontay's pale brown eyes flashed. "I don't have anything more to say to you, Laura."

Laura put a hand on her wrist, instinctively, without really knowing she was doing so. Shontay snatched her hand away.

"Don't you touch me!"

"Shontay . . . for god's sake. Please."

"Go, Laura. Go."

"I don't want to go."

Shontay looked exasperated. "I want you to."

Laura was determined not to leave. There was too much at stake. It could not end like this. She sucked up her courage and took a step forward. She raised her hand to caress Shontay's cheek, as she had done many times in the past. Shontay parried it quickly with her forearm, a slashing movement that pushed Laura's arm awkwardly to the side.

Laura's shoulders slumped. She wasn't willing to fight physically about it. She felt defeated. Willie took this opportunity to show up at the door. He recognized Laura and began rubbing against her ankle. She smiled and looked down at him, hearing him purr loudly.

"At least somebody's happy to see me."

She looked up and saw Shontay's eyes cloud over briefly, a surprise to Laura, and apparently to Shontay too since she immediately turned her head to the side and shook it, as if to clear the cobwebs. Laura quickly leaped on her advantage.

"Shontay . . . I'm not going. Not until we talk."

"You already talked. You said you were sorry. Thank you. Apology accepted."

She tried to step toward the door to open it again, but Laura blocked her way. "No . . . we have to talk more."

Shontay shook her head, her eyes again steely and fierce. Laura did not know what to do but felt something must be done, and so she stepped around her and walked into the living room, sitting down in a large, soft-upholstered easy chair that she had not noticed on her last visit. Maybe it was new. It was very comfortable, and she sank a little into the cushions, suddenly realizing that this was a disadvantageous position for her since she was slumped awkwardly in the soft chair while Shontay now loomed over her, angular and tall and imperious as ever, as she approached.

Laura struggled back up, sitting perched on the edge. But instead of confronting her, Shontay sat on the sofa across from her. Willie came in and stared back and forth at the two of them, as if not knowing which one to approach.

"You've got Willie confused," Laura said, calmly. "He thinks we're fighting. He doesn't know which one to snuggle up to. Last time he saw me we were naked and . . . you know, happy together."

Shontay scowled, as if Laura had said something obscene and loathsome. Don't remind me, her eyes said.

"I really like your new clothes," Laura said, rushing on, unwilling to let Shontay gather her anger for a new assault. "They look so stylish on you. They really show off your best features. I especially like that dress. So summery and . . . you know, bright. The bright colors look great on you."

Shontay really did look terrific, Laura thought. She might be cold and implacable, but physically she looked like a model, thin and beautiful in her bright, flowery dress, which clung around her long, thin, but very shapely legs. The ivory hue of the fabric, which was splashed with brightly colored flowers, was especially striking against Shontay's smooth, light brown skin and made her look a little darker than she really was, like rich, thick molasses.

"Thank you," Shontay swallowed uncomfortably, wary of accepting any compliments from someone as devious and treacherous as Laura. ". . . I guess. You were the one who criticized my clothes, remember?"

She said this without a trace of humor, as if she resented it deeply. And yet she *had* changed her style, and the results were undeniably successful. Laura took this contradictory signal as an encouraging sign. She hates me, but she can't forget. I made her pant.

Laura smiled at her warmly, this time genuinely forgoing all the sentimental treacle she had initially had hoped would break down Shontay's resistance.

"Can't we be friends again?" she asked, softly.

"Who said we're not friends," Shontay said, not smiling, in fact very grim.

Feeling very emboldened but still not knowing if anything would come of it, Laura stood up from the easy chair and went over to the sofa, sitting down cross-legged on the floor next to it, and next to Shontay's legs. She smiled up at Shontay and rubbed her cheek against the skirt of Shontay's summery dress, where its folds fell behind her calf.

"It smells good, too," Laura whispered. "*You* smell good."

"I think you better leave."

"You look so much more beautiful with your hair down. Why don't you take it down? Why don't you let me take it down?"

Shontay shook her head.

They did not speak for several minutes. Laura's brain was working furiously, and she wondered if Shontay's brain were scheming too. Parry . . . thrust . . . parry. Will she give in? Will she give up?

"I was looking through this big coffee table book I have about models," Shontay finally said, quietly, almost inaudibly. "I saw this picture of, what was her name, Stephanie something . . . Seymour. Stephanie Seymour. Do you know her?"

"I've never been introduced," Laura smiled.

"I mean who she is. You look just like her. She was a famous model. Probably still is, but she must be a little older now."

"You're the one who looks like the model," Laura said.

"You mean tall and skinny?" Shontay said, revealing a trace of her old bitterness.

"I mean tall and slender and impossibly beautiful," Laura said, looking up over Shontay's knees and straight into her eyes.

"That's just bullshit, Laura," Shontay said, breathing more than speaking the words. "That girl you were with was beautiful."

The knife turned in Laura's gut. She had thought they were slowly, painfully climbing out of this particular morass, and now they had fallen abruptly back into it. Instead of allowing it to happen, she charged on blithely.

"Maybe all you need is a little more meat and potatoes. Why don't you come downstairs and let me cook you a big dinner. I can cook, you know."

Shontay grinned. "I know. You helped me in the kitchen right here, don't you remember?"

"I do remember." Laura let her eyes flow and crackle with sexual innuendo. "I remember everything."

Shontay looked away. "I'm not hungry."

By this time Willie had found Laura's lap. Laura petted him in a relaxed, leisurely way and again rubbed her cheek sensually against the fabric of Shontay's dress, this time letting her cheek brush also against the smooth, warm skin of Shontay's long, shapely calf. Shontay felt it too. She pulled her leg away, not dramatically, but just far enough to make it clear to Laura what was off limits.

"I'm going to have a cigarette," Shontay said, abruptly pushing herself up from the sofa.

Laura had forgotten that Shontay smoked, especially in tense moments like this. She was a little disconsolate, sitting on the floor with her back to the sofa, petting Willie, feeling foolish. On the other hand, being at floor level gave her the opportunity to stare at Shontay's ravishing long legs as she walked across the room on her way to the kitchen to get a saucer to use for an ashtray. The skirt of her thin, flowery dress fell only to her knees, and her long, willowy, flexing brown calves were fully—gloriously—visible. Laura, as she watched the sleek muscles ripple, could not now hide from herself the distant quivering deep inside her pussy.

She fully expected Shontay to avoid the sofa when she returned, since Laura had so obviously been trying to weaken her by subtle, devious caresses, but instead she came right back with her lit cigarette and saucer to the same spot and sat down. She placed the saucer on the coffee table and expelled two long streams of tobacco smoke from her nostrils. She was nearly as stiff and contemptuous as ever, but Laura wondered if this were a sign.

Where do we go now? she wondered.

She noticed that Shontay's legs were no further away from her than they had been when she stood up, and so she scooted closer to them, readjusting Willie in her lap. She wanted more than anything to kiss one, but instead she leaned across and rubbed her cheek against Shontay's bare calf again, a caress of astonishing intimacy nevertheless, which was not lost on either of them. This time, to Laura's intense delight, Shontay did not move her leg away. Willie, however, probably tired of the maneuvering and the awkward tension between the two women, hopped off Laura's lap and began to preen himself.

Shontay continued to smoke in brusque, haughty movements, blowing smoke out of her mouth now in straight, even streams. Slowly, Laura turned her face, still rubbing her cheek against Shontay's calf muscle, until her lips grazed the girl's hard shin. Shontay didn't move. Laura let her lips slide across the shin bone and over to the curved calf muscle, pressing them lightly against it. Still, Shontay did not move.

Now Laura trailed her fingers tenderly along Shontay's bare leg, caressing it and beginning to kiss Shontay's shapely calf muscle instead of just pressing her lips against it. Now Shontay pulled her leg away, not abruptly, in fact slowly, but with definite intent.

"Don't do that."

She glowered at Laura, her head wreathed in smoked, as Laura looked up at her.

"Your legs are so beautiful," Laura said in a hushed, worshipful voice, meaning every syllable.

"They're skinny. You aren't going to start all that shit again, are you? 'You're legs are so beautiful. You're so gorgeous. Why do you cover up that beautiful body.' Just drop it, okay?"

"Okay."

Laura again scooted closer to the leg Shontay had moved away from her. Next time Shontay moved it, she would truly have to alter her position on the sofa. I'm not going to let you wiggle out of this too easily, darling, Laura thought.

She let a few moments pass, until Shontay had finished her cigarette and snuffed it out in the saucer. When Shontay again sat back, Laura again pressed her cheek against her calf.

"This is getting a little repetitious, Laura," Shontay said, unable to keep a slight trace of amusement out of her voice, but not moving her leg.

"Mmmmm, I'm sorry . . . maybe I should kiss the other one," Laura murmured softly, shifting her position so that she was angled between Shontay's legs, her lips now close to the other smooth, light-molasses colored calf.

She caressed it carefully with both hands and kissed it more ardently, moving her lips up Shontay's shapely calf to her knee, kissing it too. Shontay squirmed a little but did not stop Laura. Her thighs even yawned open slightly as if to help Laura, who obligingly moved her body up a little, planting slow, tender, but increasingly passionate kisses on the smooth inner flesh of Shontay's slender thigh. As her face rose higher, she pushed up the thin skirt of Shontay's dress to about five inches above her knees.

She turned her head and kissed the inner flesh of Shontay's other thigh too, hearing a tiny, half-concealed intake of breath as Shontay gasped. Shontay's delicious thighs were very slim, and Laura could see how she might have been teased by others about them through her no doubt gawky teenaged years: spindleshanks, stilts girl, and other stuff. But now, though thin, they were delightfully firm and shapely, warm and marvelously smooth under Laura's moving lips, the skin richly tan like pale clover honey. Laura, unable to resist, began to lick it sensually, not a major sexual uptick, but just a smooth transition from kissing to also tasting.

A soft, very distant mewling sound came from deep inside Shontay's chest, a sound she tried to conceal by swallowing and breathing more loudly, but she was unsuccessful. She did not move, however, except to open her legs a micro millimeter more for Laura.

Since every time Laura opened her mouth, she got her words flung back in her face, she now kept silent and lavished her attention on kissing Shontay's thighs, which was thrilling her so much anyway that she scarcely had energy for anything else. The feel of Shontay's warm, velvet flesh under her lips was indescribably beautiful and erotic at the same time. The long, smooth muscles of Shontay's thighs tensed, relaxed, flexed in small isolated areas as the sensations caused by Laura's lips excited them, then moved on.

Laura pushed Shontay's skirt up a little farther, moving her face up higher between Shontay's thighs. She could now see the pale green fabric of Shontay's panties in the shadowy valley of her crotch.

"Don't do that," Shontay said, squirming, trying to give her quavering voice an authority that would compel Laura to stop, but not succeeding.

"Don't you like it?" Laura asked softly.

"Yes."

"Then why do you want me to stop?"

"I . . . don't. I hate you, Laura . . . for making me . . . feel this way."

"Mmmm . . . you don't hate me," Laura murmured, her lips moving higher, higher. "You wish I would do this to you every night."

Shontay giggled softly in spite of herself. "Oh god . . . it really feels good," she panted, a trace of a smile now curving the sides of her sensual mouth as she looked down at Laura.

"I'm going to make it feel even better."

"No . . . I don't want you to."

Shontay made of a show of trying to close her legs, to push Laura out, but she was clearly not serious, and Laura gently pushed her thighs open again with her fingers, taking the opportunity to move her lips even higher, so that her mouth was now only inches from Shontay's panties. They were damp, not soggy yet, but noticeably moist, and fragrant with her flowing cunt nectars. Laura knew that Shontay's hot little slit was open and pulsing and oozing behind the thin, damp fabric, and she deliberately—certainly before Shontay had realized that any such move was likely—moved her mouth up farther, pressing her lips into Shontay's pale green panties just where they covered her pussy.

Then she breathed a slow stream of warm air through the fabric directly into Shontay's gaping, aching quim. This caused a deep quiver to roll through Shontay's long body, as if radiating out from the center, where Laura was softly blowing into her pussy through her panties, spreading through her flesh all the way from her toes to her scalp, and she even made a soft whinny as she shook, totally helpless for about three seconds.

"Oh! Don't . . . *do* that!" she gasped. "Ohhhhh!"

Laura ignored her. By now she had pushed the skirt of the flowery dress way up over Shontay's waist, exposing her whole groin. Still pressing her lips against the damp cloth of Shontay's panties, she continued to caress the tense muscles of Shontay's inner thighs with her fingertips, though by now Shontay had begun to squirm so much that gentle caresses were getting to be beside the point. She was whimpering too, though Laura could tell she was embarrassed to have yielded so easily.

"Ohhhnnnn . . . oh Laura . . . what are you doing?"

Laura said nothing. She was still forcing her warm breath through the cloth of Shontay's panties into her wet pussy, and she loved the effect it was having on the girl, who seemed to be turning to jelly before her very eyes, and under her very fingertips. Her warm breath and Shontay's wetness had made the damp cloth sag into the open groove of her pussy, forming a small indentation into which Laura could easily insinuate her tongue.

This she did without hesitation, pushing the cloth into Shontay's pussy and enjoying the tangy dew that now touched her taste buds for the first time. The thick, sweet, musky odors emanating from Shontay's excited cunt became quickly more apparent too, and Shontay stiffened, then undulated, whimpering louder, more aroused than ever.

"Unhhhhh! Oh . . . Laura . . . unnhhhhh! Oh god!"

Having finally got the upperhand, Laura was not about to relent. She did not want to pull back, then have Shontay suddenly regain her self control, shutting her legs, maybe even ordering Laura away. She also knew she had little to fear from Shontay coming too soon, because even though Shontay was clearly aroused, she did not spill over quickly, and in fact Laura was the only one who had been able to make her come, using skill and patience.

And so she worked her tongue deeper, pushing the cloth deeper between Shontay's pussy lips, and feeling the cloth become wetter too against the tip of her tongue, still breathing between Shontay's cunt lips as well as invading them with the rest of her mouth. As her tongue pushed the damp cloth deeper into Shontay's pussy, the edges of Shontay's panties began to pull in, exposing the smooth crease on each side where her thighs joined her pelvis, and also a glistening black fringe of shiny pubic hair on each side.

Laura wondered if she herself could stand the sexual excitement she was creating here. Both she and Shontay had become enveloped very suddenly in a hot cloud of seething sex, and whatever fencing and skittishness they had both displayed earlier had completely vanished. She caressed the smooth parts of Shontay's body that had appeared where her panties had pulled away, pushing the cloth even deeper into the girl's pussy with her tongue, then pressing the flat base of her tongue hard against the top where she knew Shontay's tiny, engorged clit had to be.

"Ungghhhh!" Shontay suddenly groaned.

"Oh yes," Laura heard herself murmuring, thrusting her tongue forward, waggling her head a little, letting Shontay feel the full force against her clit and the upper part of her small pussy through the wet cloth of her panties.

"Unnghhh! Laura!" she groaned again.

Now Laura pulled the wet cloth out of Shontay's pussy with her fingers, tugging it to the side, and allowed her tongue to slip directly between the slick, buttery black lips and into the shiny hot pink cleft. Shontay's body arched against the back of the sofa.

"Ohnngg! Oh shit!"

"Honey . . . honey . . ." Laura purred, slowing the pace a little, now fearing that Shontay might indeed come too quickly after all.

The girl was wildly excited, her mysterious pale brown eyes flecked with dancing sparks of sexual fire as she looked down at Laura's face in her crotch. She was so lovely and vulnerable here with her summery dress pushed up around her waist, her body lying askew across the sofa, her hair half-disheveled and beginning to fray and stick out from its tight bun, her honey golden thighs spread, her mouth slack, her eyes throbbing, her pussy wet and red and swollen, that half of Laura wanted to just go ahead and deliver the *coup de grâce* right now.

She's going to come. She's going to come hard. I can just go ahead and let it happen.

But the other half of her wanted more and had begun to form an idea. She began to pull Shontay's panties down, pushing her yawning thighs shut for a moment to get them down over her knees, then kissing her smooth belly as she pulled them off and cooing to her at the same time.

"Take this off . . ." she cooed softly, working quickly. "We'll just take all this off and . . . get it out of the way . . . yes."

As if sunk in a hypnotic trance, a deep swoon or sexual dream, Shontay moved mechanically to allow Laura to remove her panties, then her dress. Then Laura was out of her own clothes in a flash, pulling Shontay across the room to the large, overstuffed easy chair she herself had been sitting in earlier. She again marveled at Shontay's long—very long—smooth brown back as she leaned forward to unclasp her bra, skimming it off Shontay's shoulders with both hands and planting a kiss between her shoulder blades.

"This way," she coached, turning the girl and sitting her gently down in the chair. "I want you . . . oh Shontay, I want you so bad."

Shontay said nothing, panting softly, looking up at Laura obediently—so different from her usual sharp and imperious manner—as Laura placed her in the chair. Laura pulled the girl's long, angular body forward so that Shontay's perfect little rump was perched on the edge of the seat cushion, the rest of her slender torso leaning back at a forty-five degree angle into the chair. Shontay's small, delicious breasts swirled and jiggled as she settled back, and Laura could not keep herself from caressing them with her fingers, gently kneading Shontay's dark caramel nipples, wanting to suck and swallow them, but saving it for later.

"Oh Laura . . . what are we doing?" Shontay asked in a small, quavering voice, as if she were a small child embarking on a strange adventure.

"This is what we're doing," Laura chuffed, panting herself as she now spread Shontay's long legs, pushing them up and back and propping them over the arms of the chair, exposing the wet, bright pink, inflamed seam of Shontay's glistening pussy.

Her blood was racing so fast that she wondered why it didn't just gush up from her throat, or spurt out from under her fingernails. Her body was raging with hot, happy lust for this long, lovely girl, who had been so cruelly rejecting her only moments earlier. And she could see from the rapid pulsing in Shontay's magical light brown eyes that Shontay was feeling equally hot.

In one graceful motion, Laura, facing Shontay, climbed onto the chair herself, placing the crook of each knee over the chair's arms, pressing the insides of her own thighs against the yawning, uptilted backs of Shontay's sleek light brown thighs, and lowered her own throbbing, oozing pussy onto Shontay's. She grabbed the back of the chair above Shontay's head with both hands to steady herself.

"Ahhhh!" Shontay gasped as she felt Laura's wet, warm, slippery cunt flesh come into direct contact with her own.

"Oooohhhhh . . . oh god, that feels good!" Laura gasped, looking down at her, catching her eyes, letting the hot current of her lust shoot between them, and smiling inwardly as she felt Shontay's lust shoot back and intermingle with her own.

Shontay nodded, mouth open. "Oh yeah. Oh!"

With a curious smile, twisted alluringly with scorching sexuality, Shontay raised her hands to Laura's dangling breasts and began to squeeze them, twirling and pinching Laura's nipples between her thumbs and forefingers, while Laura began slowly to move her wet pussy up and down against the girl's swollen, gaping furrow. They had made love in several different ways, but their cunts had never touched until now, and Shontay's eyes quickly rolled up as the acute sensations swarmed through her body.

"Unnhhhhhh! Oh . . . oh Laura . . . ohnnnn yes!"

Their position in the chair gave Laura a kind of leverage she had never imagined before, and she could actually fuck Shontay, almost the way a man would, or the way she would with a strap-on, pumping and pushing her pussy hard into Shontay's, making Shontay whimper and her eyelids flutter with each thrust.

"Unhhh! Oh yes . . . I love it that way!" she gasped to Laura. "Oh yes, Laura! Unhhhhh!"

"Oh honey . . . I love your beautiful pussy. It feels so good against mine. Oh Shontay . . . you are so lovely. How could you think I wouldn't want you? Oh god, I want you so much!"

"Ungghh!"

"Am I doing it too hard?"

"Ungghh! No . . . oh no . . . unghhhh! You can . . . do it harder! Oh!"

There was hardly any way Laura could prevent herself from doing it harder. She was so swept up by this novel position, by Shontay's pliant and eager acceptance of it—Shontay was now enthusiastically grinding her hips and pushing her pussy up into Laura's increasingly vigorous thrusts—and by Shontay's fingers feverishly pinching her excited nipples that she could barely control the urge to send them both over the edge in a mere instant into an explosive conflagration of fiery coming.

She knew she could do it. They were both wildly aroused by this style of fucking, and Shontay was moaning and undulating under her, while Laura herself was consumed by sharp, relentless lust for the girl, jabbing and mashing her wet pussy into Shontay's, fucking her hard, and fast, with short, powerful thrusts. But she also knew that neither one of them wanted it to be over, not so fast.

"Ohhhhh . . . oh shit it's so good . . . let's slow down for a second," Laura panted.

Shontay, eyes glowing in their murky light brown depths with fierce embers, looking submissively up at her and instinctually let her body slide into the more graceful motion that Laura had adopted to slow them down.

Still holding onto the back of the chair with her hands for balance, Laura slowed the pace to a rocking, slow, delicious, rhythmic grind, arching her back so that she could push her naked breasts into Shontay's face, gasping as the girl's sensual lips chased her nipples. The thick, shiny, chestnut-colored flag of Laura's long hair fell across Shontay, who tossed her head sensually into it, as if luxuriating in the feel of it sliding across her cheeks and her forehead. The warm wet inner flesh of Laura's pussy slid across the slippery, slick, well-lubricated dark pink interior of Shontay's splayed cunt, driving them both into frenzies of sexual pleasure that made a slow, sensual rhythm less and less possible.

"Suck them harder . . ." Laura panted down to Shontay, whose mouth had caught her nipples, first one, then the other, sucking them busily but not hard enough for Laura. "Harder," Laura panted. "Do it harder . . . yes! Unhhhh!"

Shontay complied, sucking a large chunk of Laura's breast into her mouth, and moving her hands down Laura's sides to her hips at the same time, holding Laura's hips and jabbing and grinding her own cunt up faster and harder into Laura's cunt now as she sucked Laura's breast almost savagely. Laura responded by fucking her harder too, jabbing her pussy down into Shontay's, swirling her hips, jabbing again, rubbing the two hot, streaming slits together until she knew beyond doubt that both were going to simply dissolve into flames in a shattering climax in just seconds.

Oh, you're not going to have any trouble coming this time, honey, Laura thought, as she whipped them both into a keening, whimpering frenzy, fucking Shontay's pussy so hard with her own that the huge easy chair began to rock and move on the carpet. And, as if reading Laura's thoughts, Shontay began to churn and moan rapidly, in an urgent delirium of hot need, grunting softly, almost hysterically as Laura's wet nipple slipped from her mouth.

"I . . . don't know about . . . you . . ." Laura panted heavily, now ramming and rubbing Shontay's pussy roughly with her own, "but I'm . . . going to . . . come. Oh god!"

"Oh yes . . . Laura!" Shontay mewled, her head suddenly jerking to the side and her body buckling under Laura, grimacing, as if a stabbing jolt of fierce pleasure had ripped through her. "Ungghhh!"

Gripping the back of the chair in a purple passion of intense lust, Laura jammed her wet pussy into Shontay's, giving the girl several short, quick, hard, fierce rabbit jabs, bringing them both to a shockingly explosive orgasm at nearly the same instant. Actually, Laura was lucky this time since Shontay came a few seconds before she did, in contrast to the way it usually happened.

Usually Laura tried and tried to hold off but spilled over just before Shontay arrived at the finish line, which was not so bad seeing as how they both just collapsed in convulsions together. But this time, even while surging and whimpering and panting in the grip of her own sharp and urgent lust, she realized that Shontay had beat her there and was already in the grasp of an orgasmic seizure that had wrenched the breath from her body.

"Ahhnnnn . . . ahhnnnnn!" Shontay moaned helplessly under Laura in the chair.

"Oh . . . now!" Laura gasped, almost unable to get the words out reflexively as she felt sharp contractions begin deep inside her own body.

"Unnngghgh! Oh Laura! Anngghhiieeeee! Unnmmmgghaaiiiee!" Shontay wailed, suddenly stiffening, almost levitating off the chair, pushing her jerking, gyrating pelvis up into Laura's swirling groin, pushing her pussy even harder into Laura's as she came in wild, straining undulations.

"Oh yes . . . oh yes!" Laura gasped, feeling the forcible upsurge of her own climax suddenly stun her from within. "Ahhnnggggg! Oh! Ummnnghaaaiiiii! Oh shit . . . honey . . . honey!" she keened desperately, sagging down into Shontay, her body shuddering in huge convulsions as a killing orgasm shook her.

It was by far the most tumultuous, thrilling, scorching, and exhausting sexual moment they had ever shared, and Laura instinctively knew as she lay slumped and panting on top of Shontay in the chair that it had altered their relationship in ways they would not understand quickly. Shontay too was stunned and panting, her long, angular body crumpled awkwardly under Laura's, her legs still pinned up and back by Laura's thighs.

"Oh god . . . let me get off of you . . . you'll get a cramp or something," Laura finally said in a hushed, awed voice, as she crawled off the chair and helped Shontay to an upright position.

She could hardly believe what they had done, and the way they had both come so explosively. Somehow from the moment she had pushed the cloth of Shontay's panties up into Shontay's oozing pussy with her tongue, Laura realized that they had both been enveloped in a hot, swirling haze of sex so potent and magical that it had swept them with relentless forward motion to this moment of tingling afterglow and wonder. She could see that Shontay too was only now regaining her senses.

"Wow . . ." Shontay sighed softly, her pale brown eyes widening as she looked into Laura's eyes, her hair spritzing out from all sides, making her look fetchingly soft and mussed and sexy. "That must be what it feels like to get raped."

Even though both of them knew that rape was a bad thing, Shontay didn't look like she felt that a bad thing had been done to her. Quite the opposite.

Laura leaned forward and kissed her high, shiny forehead, gleaming from a thin film of sweat that they had both developed in the heat of this coupling.

"I didn't rape you," she murmured softly, caressing Shontay's cheek as she kissed her. "I fucked you . . . I was wild to fuck you . . . I couldn't stop myself."

Shontay smiled slyly. "I call it rape. And right here in my Daddy's own chair, too."

Laura embraced her, crouching on the floor in front of the chair, leaning forward and up to clasp her awkwardly, but unable to control the urge to hug her hard, luxuriating in the feel of their naked breasts finally mashing together.

"Do you think he'd be upset?" she asked. "Knowing his little girl was being fucked by a raving sex fiend . . . and a woman too . . . and a white woman . . . in his very own easy chair?"

Shontay smiled dreamily, caressing Laura's back with her long, graceful fingers. "What he doesn't know won't hurt him. I'll tell you one thing, though. I'll never be able to look at this chair in the same way again."

Laura laughed softly. Shontay nibbled her ear. It was an awkward position, though, and so she pulled Shontay back to the sofa, where they could spread out and embrace more comfortably.

"Why do you think it matters that you're white?" Shontay asked, seriously.

Laura considered it. "I guess it doesn't. I wondered if maybe it mattered to you."

Shontay looked thoughtful. "I can't say I would have ever done this with a sister, that's true," she said, reflectively.

Laura caressed her perfect collarbones with a fingertip. "You weren't really falling all over yourself to do it with me, either." She nuzzled her long brown neck. "You have the neck of a goddess."

Shontay squirmed restlessly and pulled slightly away from Laura, just enough to look her in the eyes, still very serious. Laura remembered that she had missed the signs before, the signs that Shontay had deeper feelings than she, Laura, had anticipated. She now knew to pay closer attention.

"It wasn't exactly that," Shontay said solemnly. "I was . . . afraid. I could feel myself . . . liking you. I had a couple of white girlfriends in college . . . high school, too. But not really close. We didn't really share much. And when you were up here with me, in the kitchen, I began to feel this . . . I don't know, electricity? This magnetism? And you know, the fact that you were white made it even more . . . how should I say this, mysterious? Exciting?" She raised a hand to Laura's large mane of chestnut hair. "And I wanted to touch your hair. I didn't really think about going any farther than that. Just your hair. But then I saw your eyes looking at me like . . ."

"Like this?" Laura smiled, feeling a sudden influx of renewed desire.

Shontay nodded, half-embarrassed. "Like you wanted to—"

"Fuck you?"

Shontay nodded again. "You always get me . . . with that word. We just don't use that word in my family. My parents, you know, are college professors. My mother teaches at Golden Gate, and my father is in charge of the Institute for Governmental Relations over in Berkeley. That's why they're gone . . . they went to some conference. They're always going to conferences and academic meetings. Anyway, I was brought up to . . . well, just not to use words like that."

"Should I stop using them?"

"God, it makes me so hot when you say it to me," Shontay confessed, breaking into a broad grin.

Without replying, but giving her significant look, Laura now dropped her mouth to Shontay's delicious small breasts. They were the prettiest little teacup-shaped balls of flesh, so small that when Shontay was dressed you doubted they were there. But they were perfect, capped with smallish, dark caramel colored nipples that Laura licked lovingly, slowly, sensually, while Shontay looked down at her.

"You really like them, don't you?" Shontay asked, as if unable to believe it.

This, Laura knew, was actually bait, for Shontay knew how exquisite her breasts were, and that no one would expect to find these rare beauties on such a skinny, tall girl. Laura took one small breast in both hands and sucked the entire globe into her mouth, feeling Shontay's stiffening nipple rub up against the back of her throat.

"Unhhhh!" Shontay moaned. "God, I love it when you do that!"

"Mmmm, I think we're going to end up fucking again, darling," Laura murmured to her, shifting her mouth to the other breast.

Shontay pushed her back again, before Laura could get the second breast entirely into her mouth.

"I want to . . ." she broke up in soft giggles. Then she leaned close, her wet nipples brushing against Laura's breasts, and brought her mouth up to Laura's ear, smoothing aside a large soft curtain of Laura's hair. " . . . to 'fuck' *you* this time."

"Oooohhhhh!" Laura dissolved into giggles of her own, feeling a sharp shiver of excitement that was very apparent to Shontay. "God, I can't wait. In the chair too?"

Now Shontay looked uncertain. "I was thinking of right here."

"Why not the chair?" Laura said, already sliding off the sofa and pulling Shontay with her. "Then, every time you look at it, you'll think of how we both fucked each other into the screaming meemies in it."

Shontay beamed, her tiny breasts bouncing as she followed Laura quickly. Laura turned and sank into the chair, pulling her legs up over the arms, very familiar by now with the position in which she had earlier placed Shontay. But Shontay frowned and pulled her up.

"Not so fast," she complained. "I wasn't finished kissing. I don't want to just . . . you know, fuck. I like it when we sort of . . . go slowly into it."

Laura smiled warmly. "That makes two of us," she said softly, uptilting her mouth to Shontay's.

"You're a good kisser," Shontay murmured after a minute or two of sweet, sensual tongue-intermingling.

Laura again leaned back into the chair, pulling Shontay forward on top of her, embracing her, kissing her more feverishly.

"So are you. I love the feel of your naked body against mine. I want you to fuck me so bad," she breathed into Shontay's mouth, their lips searching each other, their tongues now dancing and stabbing each other. "I want you to fuck me. Please fuck me."

Shontay was starry-eyed; there was no other way to describe it. Her eyes shone with happiness. Laura reached up.

"Only one thing I insist on," she whispered. "Take this hair down. I love it when it falls all around your face. It makes you look so sexy."

"Really?"

Shontay still had trouble sometimes believing she could be sexy. She and Laura hurriedly unfastened the pins that held her hair in place, and Shontay shook it loose. It fell in soft, dark clumps around her cheeks, and just seeing it frame her glowing, happy face seemed to ratchet up the reawakened lust in Laura's pussy a few more notches. *God, she is really lovely, she has no idea how lovely she is.*

Again Laura scooted back and lifted her body into position on the chair, spreading her thighs wide, watching Shontay's eyes dart to her now-gaping pussy, all slick and wet with fresh, aromatic juice. *Yes, honey . . . yes, honey . . . do you want my pussy?* Laura said with her eyes. *Do you want it? You can have it. Take my pussy . . . honey, take it, take my pussy.*

"Come on, you sexy devil," she teased Shontay in a low, smoking voice. "Come here and take what you want from me."

Shontay's sexy smirk grew more serious and dangerous, a change that sent a sexual charge through Laura, making her quiver excitedly inside. Shontay climbed carefully onto the arms of the chair, draping her incredibly long legs over each one, then shifting forward to bring her own pussy close to Laura's. Laura looked up at her, seizing her eyes, forcing Shontay to look deep into her own.

"Oh god, I love the feel of your pussy against mine," Laura panted.

Shontay briefly bit her full lower lip, her pale brown eyes glazing over. "Me too."

She reached forward for the top of the chair back, as Laura had done earlier, both for support and for leverage, and then brought her groin forward until her wet, warm furrow pressed firmly into Laura's. Again Laura quivered throughout her entire body. She marveled that one could feel this sensation twice in one day, relishing the hot, wet, slippery flesh of Shontay's small pussy sliding against the aching, exposed, slick inner folds of her own cunt.

She began swirling her pelvis up into Shontay even before Shontay began any motion herself. For a brief moment Shontay seemed paralyzed, or suspended in a deep, motionless trance of sexual rapture, her cunt glued to Laura's, her whole body locked in a shocking spell of intense pleasure. But then she slowly began to come back to life, swirling her hips too in slow motion with Laura, and even jabbing her pelvis forward now, as Laura had done to her earlier, and as she had told Laura she wanted to do.

"Yes!" Laura panted softly, looking up at her, watching Shontay's small, lovely breasts slide up and down her body as she slowly pumped and gyrated, running her fingers feverishly up and down

Shontay's flexing thighs, and then her long, impossibly long, smooth back. "Ohhnnnngg! Yes! Ohhnnngg yes honey . . . yes honey!"

They kept it up in a slow, grinding rhythm for a few minutes, but Laura grew dismayed as she realized she was going to climax very soon. It rarely took her very long, especially when the situation was as emotionally charged as this one, and the novel position, as well as Shontay's eagerness to be on top, combined to unleash a sharply urgent sexual response in Laura, who began whimpering and bucking under Shontay's thrusting hips, writhing in the large, soft chair, going truly wild.

"Oh! Oh!" she cried out softly, feeling herself lose control. "Oh yes, honey! Oh god . . . do it harder! Ungghhh! Yes! Ungghhh! Yes . . . that's it! Oh, I'm going to come, honey! Fuck me . . .yes . . . fuck me! Just like that . . . ungghhh! Ungghh!"

She knew the words would inflame Shontay, and they had the desired effect. Shontay was breathing hard now too but did not yet seem close to an orgasm, as Laura was. It was always a little harder for her, and Laura knew she should slow down, regain control, take it easy, bring Shontay along with her, let her concentrate instead of distracting her by lots of wild groaning and whimpering. But the words did goad Shontay into a rougher motion, and she began ramming her pussy into Laura's, and rubbing it hard up and down in the splayed crease of Laura's streaming cunt, grinding her lean, angular body down into Laura's uptilting groin, until there was absolutely no way Laura could keep the floods back.

Her body was gripped by a deep, unexpected shudder, which Shontay perceived. She paused for a micro-second, realizing that Laura was coming, then gripped the back of the chair even harder and began pumping Laura in quick, sharp jabs.

"You're . . . coming, aren't you . . . Laura?" she panted, fucking Laura very aggressively now, her long, sharp-angled body releasing a fierce, muscular power Laura had never felt until this moment.

"Ohhhh god yes!" Laura wailed, feeling the preliminary quakes of a stupendous orgasm beginning deep in her belly.

She could actually feel the slippery wet cunt honey that lubricated their two hot pussies increasing, flooding their groins, as they pushed and ground them passionately together. But it was the last surface sensation she experienced before a huge, wrenching spasm seemed to turn her inside out.

"Auunngghhhh!" she groaned, her back arching, bowing upward. "Ungghhmmnniiieeee! Oh! Unmmnnggghiiieee!"

This orgasm was much more severe and shattering than her previous one, and it seemed to rip through her flesh like a spray of red-hot nails, searing her, leaving her breathless, a whimpering mass of tingling flesh under Shontay's slowing thrusts. Laura did not know how long she was throttled and squeezed by this piercing ecstasy, but she came back to her senses to find Shontay still slowly rubbing their pussies together, not making any desperate attempt to get there herself, and realized something was wrong.

She didn't come, poor darling, she thought. She needs to come too. I just stole the show from her, that's all. Effortlessly, Laura slipped down sliding off the seat cushion of the chair but still holding Shontay in place by gently clasping the girl's narrow hips in her hands. This way she could sit on the floor with her head tilted back on the cushion, and Shontay's pretty, small, runny, puckered pussy was poised just above her mouth.

"Oh! Ohhhhh . . . Laura!" Shontay gasped, looking down, as Laura slid her tongue up between the glistening, swollen inner lips. "Unhhhh!"

She threw her head back, and her body tensed up. She's close, Laura realized. Why didn't she go for it? We could've come together, at the same time, I'll bet. Well, never mind, you're going to come now, sweetie. Hold on.

The position they were in suddenly thrilled Laura doubly when she realized she could hold Shontay's beautiful little hard round rump in both hands while she hastily and hungrily devoured the girl's streaming slit. She cupped both perfect little buns in her palms, digging her fingers into the spongy round flesh, eagerly sucking Shontay's cunt lips into her mouth, then slurping and stabbing her open slit passionately with her tongue.

It took only seconds for Shontay to lose control. She began fucking Laura's mouth with her pussy the same way she had moments ago been fucking Laura's cunt with it, grinding her wet quim down into Laura's mouth, whinnying softly as Laura's tongue slid up as far as Laura could make it go inside of her.

"Ohhnggggg! Oh god! Oh . . . oh Laura oh god oh yes unnhhhhh!"

Laura had fucked her enough to know that she sometimes had trouble getting there, but she was there now. She grasped Shontay's hard little buttocks fiercely in her hands and sucked as much of Shontay's small cunt as she could into her mouth, especially Shontay's clit, flicking it maniacally with her tongue, feeling the deep shudders begin inside the girl's long, straining body. Holding the back of the chair, which was now rocking and moving again under her thrashing, pumping body, Shontay jammed her throbbing cunt down into Laura's mouth and erupted in a shocking uprush of intense spasms.

"Ohhngghhmmnnnaauuhgghhh!" she cried out, a long, loud wail of almost unbearable rapture that filled the room and Laura's happy ears. "Ungghh! Oh! Auunngghiiiiieeeee! Oh shit . . . Laura . . ." she gasped, falling forward, her hands slipping off the top of the chair as she crumpled into an awkward heap slightly above Laura.

She dipped into a brief respite, but Laura sucked her again, squeezing her wonderful spongy cheeks, and quickly brought on another wave.

"Auungghhhhh! Oh . . . god! Oh please . . . oh Laura oh please . . . auungghhhhh! Oh yes!" Shontay whimpered, spilling over again with either the second wave of her orgasm, or with a fresh one.

Laura, smiling, could feel the pussy juices running down her chin, smearing her lips, and she wondered if she had ever been so happy to make another woman come. Certainly not happier. Letting Shontay wind down slowly, but fearing she might cramp somehow if left in this awkward position, Laura carefully extricated herself first and then gently helped Shontay to turn and sink into the soft cushions of the chair.

For several minutes neither of them could speak, following the intense physical and emotional aftermath of this heated collision. It was so still in the Gibsons' apartment that Laura could finally hear their soft breathing. They had stunned one another into silence. Shontay broke it after a few minutes, speaking so softly that Laura could barely hear her.

"I never met anybody at all like you," she said, shaking her head, the hint of a smile curling the corners of her mouth. "I . . . was determined not to talk to you. Ever again. I just wanted to forget it."

Laura, still naked as a jaybird, was sitting with her knees drawn up on the floor at the foot of the chair, her lips only inches from one of Shontay's long, slender, shapely brown legs. She leaned forward and kissed it sensually.

"How could you ever forget it?" she whispered.

Shontay continued shaking her head in disbelief. "I couldn't, I guess. I just wake up every morning wanting you to do that to me. I know . . ." she looked away, embarrassed, "you didn't learn how to do that by yourself. But when I saw you with her—"

Shontay's eyes clouded up briefly, and she looked away. Laura, rising up herself, took her hand and pulled her up out of the chair.

"Come over here again and cuddle with me," she said, drawing Shontay back to the sofa.

Shontay giggled and wiped away a minor tear. "This is where we started," she laughed. "Before we went to the chair. It's starting all over again."

"I promise to behave." They snuggled and nuzzled each other. "Why didn't you come with me . . . I mean, when you got me going like that?" Laura whispered, stroking her pretty little naked ass.

"I don't know. I think maybe I was just so astonished by the way you just . . . went off. So quick. And I was enjoying the feel of it. And I kind of . . . missed the moment, I guess." She smiled and kissed Laura's mouth very emotionally. "But it was all worth it because of what happened next."

"You raped my pussy and my mouth. God, it was wonderful. Let's do it again."

"Could we fix something to eat first? All this . . . 'fucking' . . . makes me kind of hungry."

Shontay looked like she was going to blush. She was demure, coy, flirtatious. Laura had never seen her quite like this. She got to her feet and pulled Shontay up off the sofa, embracing her long, naked body, tilting her head up to kiss her again.

"You are very tall," she said. "My mouth is closer to your breasts than it is to your mouth, unless I stand on my tippy toes."

Shontay smirked. "You can kiss them too," she breathed. "Whenever you want to."

Laura considered it. "Come with me. I'm going to take you downstairs like I promised and feed you some meat and potatoes. I've got two New York strip steaks just waiting for us."

"Two? Were you expecting someone?"

Laura almost laughed. Here they both were stark naked, standing in the middle of Shontay's parents' apartment, having just fucked one another silly twice in her Daddy's easy chair, sparring about food and Laura's other lovers.

"I bought them on the way home," Laura said with a stern face. "I always buy two and freeze one. I just haven't popped it in the freezer yet. What . . . are you refusing free food?"

Wide-eyed and solemn, Shontay shook her head. "I wouldn't think of it. Can I feed Willie first?"

They spotted Willie by the fireplace, looking at them as if they were aliens from another planet.

"I think we might have scared him," Laura said.

"If you ask me, he's getting used to it," Shontay said, sassily. "Every time you appear, we wind up getting naked and moaning and screaming."

"Mmmm," Laura teased her, "maybe he likes the looks of you naked. I sure do."

"Don't be nasty," Shontay smirked. She reached down and retrieved some of her clothes and some of Laura's. "Cover up. I think he likes *you* better. It's all that hair that's got him."

Laura pinned her against the wall again before they left the Gibsons' apartment. She kissed Shontay's neck and ran one hand up her thigh, under her dress, to her ass, squeezing one firm round cheek through her panties.

"I may not let you get away without . . . you know what," she murmured. "You drive me wild with desire."

Shontay trembled but summoned up enough of her old steel for a sharp reply. "Careful what you wish for, girl," she breathed.

* * *

Hot Lesbian Erotica

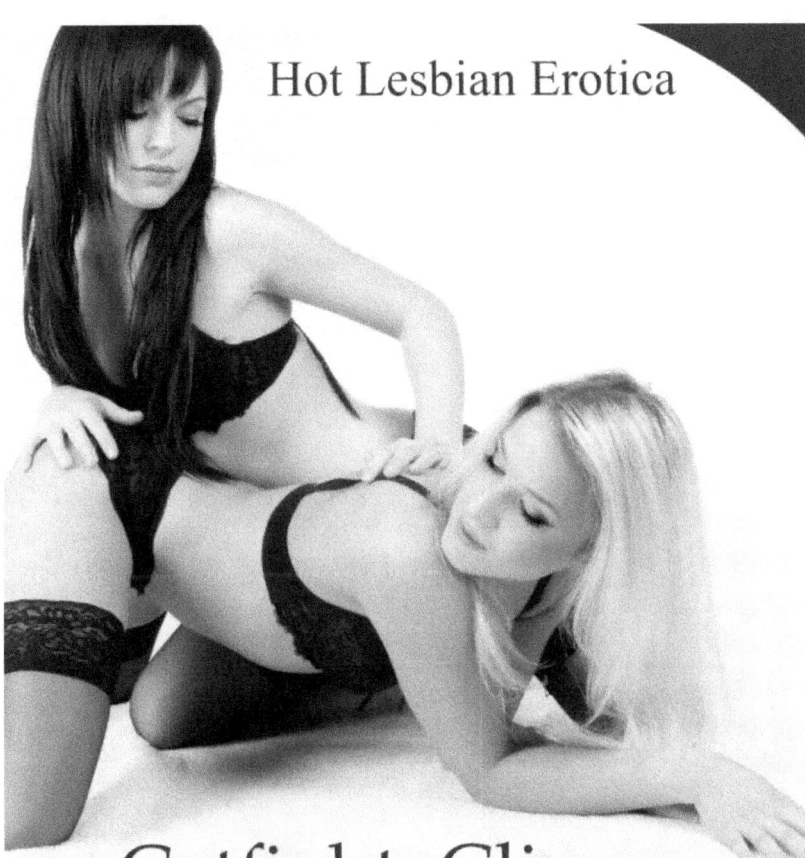

Catfight, Climax,
Friends Again
by. Miranda Mars

The Laura and
Shontay Chronicles **Part 2**

Laura heard something upstairs.

She knew the Gibsons were gone since she had seen them out the window as they were leaving earlier that day, getting into an airport shuttle with several pieces of luggage. That could mean only one thing: Shontay. When her folks were gone, she came over to feed their cat Willie and spend a little time with him. She was up there. She should've taken off her shoes, if she didn't want me to hear her, Laura thought. Maybe she doesn't realize how these old apartments telegraph every little thing.

Shontay still had not phoned Laura. Let's see, it must be almost ten days or so since she called, Laura thought, counting back. Very odd. Something's going on. They told her about the screaming and groaning down here, I'll bet, she thought, glumly.

Laura had been in such a flutter of love and exuberant sexual happiness following her night with Sara that almost nothing else had got her attention for days. On top of that, she had engaged a real estate person—a friend of Rhonda's—who had within days found her a delightful condo nestled in a forested slope on the western side of the lower Twin Peaks area. It was heavily wooded and could be foggy at times, but it was fairly new, only one previous owner, and secure and private.

Laura had made clear to the agent that, as she had put it, she couldn't bear listening to other people's noises, dogs, odious rock music, quarrels, and that that was the reason she was moving in the first place. They performed, with the cooperation of Laura's potential neighbors, several experiments to detect how soundproof these condos were, and Laura was tickled to find that someone playing heavy metal at an ear-shattering volume directly next door might as well be on the moon.

"You could commit murder in here and never be discovered until the smells started emanating," the real estate guy, a dour old man with a huge distended belly and rheumy yellow eyes, said to her, winking.

"No murders," Laura winked back. Even though he was sort of grotesque, she liked him. In fact, she loved him for finding this condo. "I meditate a lot, though. And do my yoga." It was so much fun to make up outlandish stories for strangers.

Her instant offer had been accepted, and the deal was already in escrow. As she looked around her Russian Hill apartment, especially at the view from the windows while sitting in the white sofa (where I've devoured so many lovely girls, she reflected, feeling her pussy tingle happily at the memory), she felt a little sad. You could see the Bay Bridge, and the fog swooping and swirling in over San Francisco Bay. The lights winked on everywhere, and you could even see Berkeley across the Bay when there was no fog. To the left was El Cerrito, where Jane and Kendra were now living. To the right was Oakland, where April lived. Where she's probably churning and groaning on top of that delicious Yolanda at this very moment, Laura thought, enviously. April's new girlfriend. Everybody needed a girlfriend.

The apartment had memories. Most of them were almost unbearably sweet. She would hate to leave it, but one had to move on. It would be such bliss to be able to relax in bed with Sara, say, in her new condo, and do whatever they liked without fear of eavesdropping. The thought of Sara brought her full circle to her obsession of the past few days, since she could not shake Sara out of her mind now, or the memory of Sara's caresses from her body either, or her funny faces, or her big soft black nipples, or her twinkling little silvery pussy ring.

And then she heard another very faint noise from upstairs and realized that Shontay was still there. And avoiding me, she thought. Since they had become lovers, Shontay would always ring Laura's buzzer whenever she came by to feed Willie, if her parents were traveling. But not tonight.

She is so jealous, Laura thought. Even just seeing me that time in the hall with Randi was enough to set her off. Think of what she must be feeling if her mother told her that the slut downstairs was having loud orgies with other women. Other black women. She wouldn't be able to let on anything, and it would kill her. She would be afraid of what her mother would think if she knew Shontay was one of those 'other women,' and she would also be filled with fury at Laura for violating their intimacy by daring to sleep with others.

This was a quandary Laura could appreciate. Understanding the depth of her own jealousies very well, she could empathize deeply with anyone who felt pangs of fierce resentment at the thought of someone else sharing the kind of physical intensity and rare ecstasy that Shontay and Laura had shared. It hurts, Laura thought. It really hurts. No wonder she feels that way.

Laura felt her own eyes glimmering with involuntary tears as she stood looking out her window, which she now knew she would be doing only a few more times. No views behind Twin Peaks, she thought. Oh, maybe a few nice trees. No city lights, though. I've got to go up there and talk to her. I've got to make her see that it doesn't make me care for her any less. I know how hurt she is. I know how she loves me to make love to her.

Sucking back her incipient tears, wiping the corners of her eyes with her wrist, she went quickly, before she could second-guess herself, snatching up her door key and sticking it into her bra for safe-keeping. In only a few more seconds, she was knocking on the Gibsons' door, remembering the last time she had done this, when Shontay had been so cold, and Laura had nearly raped her in Mr. Gibson's easy chair.

She had to stand a long time at the door, after knocking. Shontay was inside, she was sure of it, but Shontay knew, as Laura always did, that this wasn't the knock of some stranger handing out *WatchTowers*, as Jane had once suggested. She knows it has to be me. Either she's just trying to see if I'll give up and go away, or she's purposely making me squirm.

Laura knocked again, louder. Again she waited, but not as long this time. The door finally opened. Shontay did not open it only a crack, as she had done the first time.

Instead, she was bristling and hostile and opened it quite widely. She was drawn up to her full height, at least four inches taller than Laura, and her mysterious pale brown eyes, usually so mesmerizing and fascinating, glowed with anger like fierce hot embers.

"Oh . . . hi. It's me," Laura said clumsily, suddenly awkward and nervous.

"What do you want?"

"I . . ."

Laura was overcome by a hot welter of contradictory feelings. For one thing, Shontay was like two different people to her. Now, for instance, she had dropped her hair, which fell in loose clumped strands around her neck and shoulders, immeasurably softening her usual hard, imperious expression. She was enchanting like this to Laura, and physically desirable, since at work Shontay always had her hair pulled back tightly, severely, almost militarily, making her small, well-shaped head look even more regal on top of her elegant swan's neck. But she took it down when she and Laura went to bed, and that seemed to release a vulnerability in her that she never showed anywhere else, as well as a deep sensuality that Laura had exploited with careful skill.

But now . . .

She had her hair down, but the look in her eyes spelled disaster, not delicious sex. Shontay was tense with fury. It was very hard for Laura to respond to the threat as well as her own desire at the same time. God, I'm always a hopeless sucker for her when she gets this cold, aloof, imperial manner, she realized. It's her 'Off with your head!'' manner. I want to drag her down on the floor and do everything to her.

"I . . . just wanted to say hello," Laura gulped.

Shontay glowered and started to close the door.

"No . . ." Laura said quickly, pushing it back open a little with the palm of one hand. "Please."

"Go away, Laura."

Laura gave Shontay her own most melting look. Shontay, I adore you, I want you, I hunger for you, for your flesh, for your wonderful long lean body, for your mouth, for your sweet little pussy, for your touch, your kiss, your low murmurs, your screams when you come. I want you. Can you see that? I want to make it up to you. I'm sorry you're hurt, but I can't help that. Let me make it better. At least for a while.

Laura shook her head.

"Then you're going to lose your fingers," Shontay snapped, trying to close the door again more forcefully.

Again, Laura had to catch it with her palm and push it back. Suddenly, they were in a struggle with the door, Shontay trying to slam it shut, Laura trying to stop her.

Laura pushed it back open with such vehemence that Shontay momentarily stumbled backward, losing her grip on the knob. Laura, in turn, stumbled forward, through the door frame, one leg into the Gibsons' apartment.

"Get out of here, you bitch!" Shontay scowled, quickly recovering her balance and grabbing Laura's elbow, trying to force her back out into the hallway.

Laura didn't budge. In fact, she pushed forward, grabbing the doorjamb for leverage. "No . . . I want to talk to you."

"You ain't got a fucking thing to say to me that I want to hear," Shontay panted, now grabbing Laura with her other hand too, trying to force her back out. "Get out of here!"

Laura relaxed and straightened up, releasing her grip on the door frame, trying to step back slowly, with dignity, giving in. It wasn't worth fighting over. She let herself be pushed back beyond the door, into the hall. She could feel the tears coming to her eyes again. Shontay's face was shockingly ugly with rage.

"I can explain," she said softly, wondering what she meant by that. What could she explain that would change Shontay's feelings?

"You can't explain shit!" Shontay spat.

"I . . . I really care about you," Laura said feebly.

"The fuck you do," Shontay hissed. "You care about black cunt, that's all."

Laura's eyes widened with indignation. "How can you say—"

"Fuck off, Laura. Go find that little teeny bopper with the braids. I'll be leaving soon. I just fed Willie. I'll be gone. You can scream and holler all you want down there. Won't be anyone here to hear you."

"Shon—"

Laura started to raise two fingers to Shontay's face, to caress her cheek, as she often did in moments of tenderness. Shontay's hand came up, and Laura was afraid she was going to knock her own hand aside. Instead, Shontay slapped her hard on the cheek, a ferocious slap, so hard that the force of it swiveled Laura's head to the side. Her palm against Laura's face made a loud crack.

Laura was so surprised that the pain did not even register for a few seconds. Stunned and hurt, she suddenly felt it flame up in her face, felt real, hot tears now spring to her eyes as she staggered slightly back, raising her fingers to her cheek. Then, to Laura's own secret horror, as if it had a life of its own, her hand lashed out and up, slapping Shontay's face equally hard, with a sharp crack too.

"Ynnnee!" Shontay yelped in shock, jumping back, dropping the doorknob, as her own head jerked to the side. She raised her fingertips to her cheek. "Oh . . . you cunt!"

Now Laura was back through the open door, into the apartment, shutting it quickly behind her as Shontay backed away further, instinctively, as if preparing for another blow. But Laura, already appalled at what she had done, had no intention of striking her again.

"Listen to me . . ." she said, trying to lower her voice, make it soothing.

"Fuck you!" Shontay swore, eyes burning, body tense, angular, and sharp, twitching with fury.

"Shontay . . . listen to me," Laura said softly, advancing.

But this time, Shontay did not give ground. She shook her head, eyes blazing red instead of pale brown now, her mouth a slash of hatred. Instead of falling back more, she advanced on Laura.

"Get out!"

Though very tall and skinny, Shontay was physically imposing merely because of her height, and she was, Laura realized, very much stronger than she looked, with a wiry, tensile force that could easily be underestimated. Without warning, she grabbed Laura's shoulders and slammed Laura back into the door.

The breath nearly left Laura's body. She could feel it being crushed out of her lungs by the impact, expelled from her throat, leaving her completely stunned and bent half over.

"Wait a . . . wait a minute," she cawed, gagging softly, gulping for breath.

"I . . . ain't . . . waiting for . . . nothing!" Shontay gasped as she grabbed Laura's arms, wrenching them, grabbing at the same time for the doorknob, slamming Laura back into the door again with a fierce frontal body block.

Of course the fact that she had Laura pinned back against the door made it hard for her to open it at the same time. Even though she was out of breath and struggling hard with Shontay, Laura realized bizarrely, that this was true, as well as the fact that Shontay, now fiercely agitated, had dropped into a kind of loose and vitriolic slang she would ordinarily avoid at all costs.

At the same time, in a split second, she was very aware of Shontay's scent, the fresh, sensual odor of her body, and her hair, which brushed Laura's cheek as Shontay shoved her violently around. Just as she had responded so sharply to Sara's fresh, unique bodily fragrance, she now found herself mesmerized by Shontay's, a scent different from Sara's but so familiar and erotic that she realized she was becoming aroused even as they were fighting.

Why am I smelling her delicious fragrance when she's trying to kill me?! Laura wondered, desperately, trying to slide to the side to avoid Shontay's angular elbows and knees.

"Get the fuck out of here, you bitch!" Shontay swore, yanking Laura forward by one wrist now so that she could get the door open.

Reaching out only to keep her balance, Laura's fingers caught in the collar of Shontay's shirt, and as Shontay elbowed her roughly to the side, the fabric ripped and the buttons popped off all in one motion. Laura was left with a handful of cloth, still half-attached to Shontay's body, buttons clattering as they hit the floor.

Shontay's delicious, smooth, light brown skin was visible through the jagged rips in her shirt, and the shiny violet sateen fabric of her bra also showed. She looked down at her torn shirt in disbelief.

"Oh god, you little shit, Laura, it's my favorite blouse!" she screamed, lashing out with her hand again, the back of it this time, her knuckles catching Laura along the jaw, not a direct impact but enough to send her to her knees.

This time, Laura was a little dizzy, but she somehow felt, looking up into Shontay's blazing eyes, that Shontay too was feeling the strange, potent mixture of anger and sexual excitement that Laura was feeling. And she could also see in Shontay's eyes that she too felt it and knew Laura recognized it, and that she was implacably determined not to let it go any farther.

Shontay stumbled and lurched toward the door again, reaching for the knob, but Laura now, really for the first time, grabbed her, wrapping both arms around one of Shontay's legs to keep her from moving. Shontay was wearing pants, but Laura could feel the coiled strength of her leg under the cloth, flexing and straining, as she held on, pulling Shontay back, whimpering and trying to reason with her at the same time.

"Listen to me . . . damn you!" she hissed, barely able to speak from shortness of breath. "I want to . . . apologize."

"Fuck you!" Shontay swore, her lovely face grimacing in hatred. "Get out of here! I'm going to call the cops! Get out of here . . . you don't have my permission to be here . . . you're breaking and entering! You despicable slut, you whore, you fucking dyke! I hate you!"

Laura was desolated by these accusations. Feeling defeated and sickened, she relaxed her grip on Shontay's leg, almost ready to give in completely and leave. But Shontay was still so stiff with rage that she again stumbled, reaching for the doorknob, and her leg still entangled in Laura's arms, she fell to the floor beside Laura, an awkward heap of limbs and knobby elbows and knees, squealing a little with surprise as she fell.

"Ynnneeeee! Oh!" she yelped, twisting to free her leg from Laura's grasp. "Let me go, you cunt!"

Laura clenched her teeth, glaring at Shontay. "Quit calling me those names!"

"Fuck you!"

Eyes blazing, Shontay again lashed out with her hand, smacking Laura hard against the side of the head, aiming for her cheek but missing. Instinctively, Laura leaned forward, extending both arms, reaching with her hands for Shontay's long, exquisite neck. She had never choked anyone in her life, but something in her drove her to do it at this instant. She grabbed Shontay's neck with both hands, pushing her back, lunging over her, not really wanting to strangle or kill her but to threaten her seriously enough to make her stop.

Shontay's hands flailed at her back, pounding Laura, pummeling her wildly.

"Ungghh! Let me go! You . . . you fucking . . . you—"

But now Laura's own retaliatory fury was in gear, and she could feel a hot, sharp energy of defensive anger flood her own body. Continuing to push Shontay down, down onto her back, her fingers closed around the girl's long, beautiful neck. She did not close them tightly, though. The feel of Shontay's smooth, warm skin under her fingers was a much too sensual drug. She had kissed this beautiful swan's neck so often, and whimpered into it when coming deliriously in Shontay's arms.

"Oh god . . . you are such a cunt!" Shontay panted, struggling under Laura, rolling and pitching back and forth, trying to throw Laura off.

Her hands found their way under Laura's sweatshirt, and she clawed Laura's back, chuffing and gasping and churning desperately. God, it's almost like we were fucking, Laura realized.

"Ouchhhh! Laura yelped, tightening her fingers now on Shontay's lovely throat to make her stop. "Don't do that. Don't hurt me."

"Fuck you!" Shontay glowered up at her. "Didn't you hear me? Fuck you! FUCK YOU!"

But even though she was digging and clawing at Laura's naked back, she was not doing it the way Randi or Sholandra had once done. Her fingernails were not breaking Laura's skin. Maybe she thinks I'm going to strangle her, Laura thought. Or maybe she's feeling something like I am, like this is almost like fucking.

Laura loosened her grip, melting. I want her. Oh god, I never wanted her as much as this! I wonder if she feels that way too. She realized that her own pussy was burbling and flooding with juice. The wetness in her crotch was amazing. I wonder if she . . .

They were still tussling and struggling and panting on the floor, and Laura purposely let Shontay roll her to the side, off her body, so that she could maneuver one hand down in the vicinity of her thighs. Even though Shontay was wearing jeans, she was evidently creaming so much that the damp dew on the denim over her crotch was unmistakable as Laura's fingertips grazed it.

It was really all Laura needed to know. She had found it hard to keep her mouth off Shontay's alluring, exposed, light caramel skin up until now, and now she gave in to the impulse, leaning closer, mashing her lips aggressively into Shontay's bare shoulder, just above her shoulder blade, through a gap in her torn shirt. Laura ran her lips hungrily all over it, then across another torn strip of fabric up to Shontay's long neck, kissing it too passionately.

"Ohhnnnn!" Shontay cried out in her fury. "Ummmmggghh!"

Laura could feel her body quiver, though whether it was from sexual arousal or fresh rage she couldn't tell. But it didn't take long to find out.

"Arrngghhhh!" Shontay grunted loudly, flinging Laura off her body with almost supernatural strength, extending her arms and violently pushing Laura away. "Let go of me, you cunt! You dyke, you fucking perverted dyke! Let go of me! God, I hate you! I hate you!"

But, knowing that Shontay was aroused too, Laura was not about to give in now. True, Shontay had swelled up with a new hot bubble of fury, her pale brown eyes fiery and flaming with ferocity, her body— wildly desirable to Laura now that her shirt hung in tatters around her smooth, exposed flesh, her hair mussed and askew—stiff and tense with anger.

"I want you," Laura said, very softly, her eyes pleading. "I'm sorry. I want you."

"I hate you!" Shontay screamed. "I don't ever want you to touch me again!"

Laura knew that if she didn't overpower her, there was a lot of danger waiting for her in those long, flailing arms and legs. With a swift, gliding move, she leaned forward and again pushed Shontay onto her back, sliding one of her own thighs between Shontay's, and pulling off the shredded blouse as much as she could, pressing her lips to Shontay's half-naked body everywhere she could.

She brought her thigh up quickly and pushed it into Shontay's crotch, writhing with her, groping, sucking her long, exquisite neck.

"Oh! Oh!" Shontay whimpered, trying to free herself, but not half as hard as she had tried earlier.

Laura was wearing a sweatshirt, which was hard to tear or rip off, but Shontay's scrabbling fingers tore at it anyway, now pulling it up. Her hands raced frantically over Laura's bare skin, as if she could not make up her mind whether to scratch or caress Laura. Her quick, darting fingers pulled up the cups from Laura's bra, freeing Laura's breasts. She grabbed and twisted Laura's nipples sharply.

"Aiieeee!" Laura cried out, feeling stabbing flames shoot through her nipples and her breasts.

It was a violent attack, but it was, she knew, also very close to what they might do together sexually. She and Shontay had never indulged in the semi-rough sex that Laura had frequently experienced with some others, but what was this moment if not a sexual collision of the most acute kind?

"Oh shit . . . that hurts!" Laura glowered at her, eyes watering. "Get off me, you cunt!"

Laura slapped her. Up until now she had not struck back except in self-defense, but this time her hand flew up automatically, cracking Shontay alongside the jaw. Shontay was still lying half under her, and she was so stunned by the slap that Laura tore the remnants of her blouse away with little trouble, ripping it up, grabbing Shontay's bare shoulders, her frenzied fingers pulling and tearing at Shontay's bra straps at the same time.

Shontay's eyes, already hot with anger, suddenly flared with a thermonuclear fire that Laura had not seen there before. Reaching up with both long arms, she grabbed thick fistfuls of Laura's hair in both hands and yanked it hard. Laura's scalp exploded in pain, but it was a pain of a different quality than Shontay had probably intended. It hurt like hell, but since her experiences with Dawn and Deshona, it also was a sexual turn-on of colossal dimensions, and Laura could feel her whole body suddenly run with flame, her pussy throbbing wildly.

"Annniieeeee!" she heard herself shrieking and squealing. "Oh god . . . you bitch . . . Shontay, you bitch, let go!"

Her eyes were blurred with pain as the two of them now rolled and thrashed around on the floor as Laura tried to loosen Shontay's grip on her hair, but she could now get her hands on Shontay's beautiful violet-colored bra without obstruction. It was a pity to destroy underwear so beautiful, but without remorse, Laura tore it from Shontay's body with two violent jerks. The snaps in the back popped, and the bra simply crumpled in her hands.

"Oh shit . . ." Shontay gasped, looking down as her small, naked, teacup-shaped breasts and glimmering dark caramel nipples came into view, swaying and jiggling as she struggled with Laura.

Shontay was still yanking Laura's hair, but Laura was all over Shontay's naked upper body in a flash, squeezing her small breasts, pinching her nipples, though not as sharply as Shontay had pinched hers, then sucking them voraciously, hungrily, yelping at first as Shontay took a few more hard pulls of her hair, then groaning softly and sucking hard.

"Oh! Oh!" Shontay gulped, quickly overcome by Laura's fierce passion, her fingers relaxing, releasing the clumps of Laura's hair she had been pulling. "Ohhhnnnnn . . . oh god!"

This brief second of relaxation on Shontay's part gave Laura the chance to unfasten the zipper of the girl's jeans, while she was still hungrily sucking and mouth-mauling Shontay's nipples, and in the midst of doing it she realized that Shontay was really not resisting any longer. She even lifted her butt a little as Laura pulled the jeans over her hips and down her legs, now slipping lower, kissing her heaving stomach, running her lips all over the smooth, quivering muscles and lovely warm light brown skin.

Shontay's hands were plucking spastically at the shoulders of Laura's sweatshirt, pulling it up, as if she were trying to get it off too, and Laura quickly obliged her by hurriedly lifting it over her head and throwing it across the small entryway. As she hurriedly unfastened her scrunched-up bra, which Shontay had roughly pulled up to expose her breasts, she heard the door key she had hidden there clatter against the hardwood floor as it fell. Quickly Shontay's own fingers ran feverishly over Laura's skin too, digging into Laura's flesh.

Laura slid up again, sucking her neck, kissing her ear, her cheek, her jaw, gently pinching Shontay's saliva-wet nipples.

"I want you," she breathed.

"Fuck you," Shontay glowered at her, turning her head. "Don't you touch me."

"What if I do?"

"I'll kill you." Shontay slid the fingers of both hands into Laura's hair again as a threat.

"I'll fuck you."

"I'll kill you. You cunt."

She bucked her body, trying to throw Laura off, pulling Laura's hair again too, but not as roughly as before. Laura was very preoccupied in struggling out of her own jeans, and her panties, but she cried out as the fiery pain in her scalp flared yet again.

"Ohhnnnggaaiiieeee! Oh shit! Don't you ever stop? Owwwwwcchhh! That hurts!"

"Get off me . . . you cunt."

By now they were both completely naked, except for Shontay's panties, pale violet beauties that matched the bra Laura had destroyed. Laura slid her hands down the girl's long, smooth body to them, but immediately Shontay tightened her grip on Laura's hair, actually yanking Laura's head up so that Laura was face to face with her.

"Don't you touch me," she warned.

Looking directly into her eyes, Laura slid her fingers under the elastic band, down to one of Shontay's gorgeous tight little hard round buns. She cradled it in her palm, squeezing it gently. She could even feel a little warm cunt juice from Shontay's inflamed quim dripping down onto this delightful ripe globe of flesh, which moistened her fingers.

Oh god, she wants it as much as I do! Laura realized.

She leaned forward again, mashing the entire length of her naked body into Shontay's, noticing that she had left a little mark on Shontay's long, spectacular neck earlier, sucking it again in the same spot, sucking harder this time, so that Shontay began to squirm again under her, and again relaxed her fingers in Laura's hair.

"Unhhh! Don't do that! Unhhh! Laura . . . stop . . ."

"You . . . want it," Laura panted. "Just like . . . me."

"No," Shontay gasped, now panting too, still struggling under Laura, but writhing excitedly more than trying to escape. "No . . . don't touch me . . . ohhhhhh!"

Laura breathed a hot stream of air into her ear. At the same time, she pulled Shontay's panties down, down, down her thighs, down to her knees, which required her momentarily to slide further down the girl's long body. Shontay's long, scissoring legs were like the blades of some deadly piece of machinery, kicking and jerking at intervals up into the air.

Laura slid down, pinning the girl's thrashing legs under her, and forcibly tore Shontay's panties down and off her feet. Oh god, I want to eat her pussy, she realized, suddenly inhaling the hot, pungent odors of Shontay's aroused slit, but she knew it was too risky, since Shontay was still seething with anger. Instead, Laura slid back up, embracing her, pinning her to the floor, but dropping one hand again to Shontay's thighs, dipping it between them.

"Laura, don't you touch me!" Shontay whimpered, suddenly letting her torso fall back to the floor, her fingers now running in a frenzy over Laura's bare shoulders, then digging into Laura's back. "Don't you touch me! No!"

Laura slid two fingers up into the soupy crease of Shontay's sweet, small pussy almost before Shontay knew what was happening.

"Ahhnngggg!" Shontay gagged softly, arching her back slightly so that her small, lovely breasts bobbed in circles.

Even though they had shared some hot sex, Laura knew Shontay had never been this wet before. Not with me, at least. God, she's flooding, Laura thought. Her fingers were slathered with warm slippery fluids as she twisted them inside the tight, warm, very wet channel. Gee, I could fist fuck her, Laura thought, but knew she had better not. It was bad enough that they had struggled so hard to get to this point without adding a fresh perversity to shock and repel Shontay further.

But she didn't mind taunting her a little.

"You want me to fuck you," she chanted softly, beginning to move her hand, to rub one knuckle up against Shontay's clit, to apply clever pressure that would increase Shontay's need.

"No," Shontay gasped, shaking her head vigorously, frowning.

"You want to fuck me too," Laura chanted, feeling a very strong fluttering and hot pulsing in her own cunt, wanting desperately for Shontay to touch it too, so they could both dissolve into a molten frenzy of fucking she knew they each needed terribly.

She felt Shontay's fingernails against the bare flesh of her thigh and for a second wondered if Shontay were going to scratch her. But then she opened her thighs a little, rolling sideways partially off Shontay's body, so that Shontay could get her hand into the right position. And then . . .

She felt one of Shontay's long, thin fingers slip between her pussy lips, then slide up inside.

"Oh god . . . yes! Unhhhhh! Oh yes, honey . . . fuck me too, yes!"

But Shontay, even though she now had her finger in Laura's pussy too, refused to acknowledge in her facial expression that anything had changed. Her pale, mysterious brown eyes throbbed, though, seeming to reflect a deeper sexual trance, but she continued to shake her head slowly from side to side. Laura believed it was now okay to kiss her, and she did so without any warning, not wanting to give Shontay a chance to turn her head away or otherwise repulse her.

She leaned forward quickly and caught Shontay's mouth with her own, kissing her savagely, forcing her tongue between Shontay's sensual lips and now sliding her fingers up the girl's clit, rubbing it in tight, rapid swirls in exactly the way she had seen Shontay do herself when masturbating. It was a scorching, direct assault. With her free hand, Laura reached down again and cupped one of Shontay's small, firm buns, digging her fingertips into the warm, smooth, spongy flesh.

"Oh!" Shontay whimpered. "Oh . . . Laura!" she murmured against Laura's devouring mouth.

Laura did not let her speak. Again, she forced her tongue deep into Shontay's mouth, now gyrating her own hips so that Shontay's hand had to move in her own crotch, whether Shontay wanted to move it or not. Now, Laura exulted, they were fucking. You couldn't call it anything else, and she could feel Shontay's body beginning to undulate and squirm in spite of herself.

Laura rolled on top of her again and began to screw her in earnest now, dropping her mouth to Shontay's dark caramel nipples, her lips tearing at them, her hand plunging, swirling, rubbing, as she heard Shontay's whimpers growing more desperate and felt her body straining and churning. This moment of snuffling and soft groaning and squirming, rubbing their naked bodies together, seemed to be suspended in time for Laura, who wanted it never to end and allowed herself to experience each infinitesimal twinge and pulse of her own body and Shontay's, luxuriating in the feel of Shontay's silky wet pussy flesh against her probing fingers, loving the soft chewy sensation of Shontay's stiffening nipples against her tongue.

"Oh yes . . . honey . . . oh yes, honey," Laura purred, panting, sucking, again running her free hand up Shontay's body to her face, interlacing her fingers now in Shontay's hair, even pulling it slightly, not hard, but almost a reminder of the way she had pulled Laura's.

Shontay, though her eyes were pulsing and throbbing in the slow whirl of a gathering sexual storm, focused them on Laura for a second and lifted her hand too, sliding her long thin fingers again into Laura's hair.

"Yes . . ." Laura murmured, wildly excited, suddenly feeling a few preliminary twinges of her own coming orgasm in her pussy, which

Shontay was now rubbing and fucking more deliberately. "Yes . . . pull my hair," she glowered at Shontay, a threat, a plea, a promise.

Shontay bit her lower lip, panting, her eyelids fluttering, her pelvis swirling and bucking under Laura's body. "I . . . hate you," she gulped, glaring at Laura, then groaning softly as her eyes rolled up. "I hate you . . . Laura . . . unngghhh! Oh god!"

"Yes!"

"Unh! Unh!"

Shontay almost lost control, but then quickly recovered, tightening her grip on her fistfuls of Laura's hair. With two fingers sunk in the girl's warm, buttery slit, her palm facing Shontay's pubic bone, Laura scissored Shontay's clitoral hood between her forefinger and middle finger and began to rub up and down, forcibly, passionately, sucking her neck again, and softly whinnying as her own climax began to overwhelm her.

"Oh Shontay!"

"Ungghh! I . . . hate you! Ungghhh!"

Laura began to come and yanked Shontay's hair in her hand, sharply, for the first time. She knew Shontay would come any second too, and this would probably tip her over the edge. She could see the fires leap up in Shontay's shocked eyes as the pain hit her. Then Laura could feel Shontay's grip tightening even further.

"Auungghgghh!" Laura cried out in a wild shriek of mingled pain and sexual exuberance as she felt Shontay pull her hair in a violent yank.

A surging, roiling orgasm wrenched her body, but through it she could hear Shontay's ecstatic groaning and feel her gyrating hips almost rising off the floor, shuddering, bucking, as Shontay too erupted in a thrilling climax right behind her.

"Ohhnnmmmgggiiieee!" Shontay squealed, writhing in a fierce seizure of ecstasy under Laura, her hands both pulling Laura's hair still with amazing strength, sparking to life new hot jolts of coming in Laura's throbbing pussy.

Laura, on the other hand, released Shontay's hair at this moment, letting her hand fall to the girl's lovely bare shoulders instead, then caressing her neck, where, even in her stunned and throbbing condition, she noticed the dark, speckled blood blotch she had raised on the smooth, light brown column of beautiful flesh. Oh god, now she'll hate me even more, she thought, hearing Shontay's labored breathing in her ear, feeling Shontay's long, lithe body begin to relax as the last twitches of her orgasm died away.

Finally, Shontay too released Laura's hair, which now fell in a large, shiny flag over her face as Laura slowly drew her body up to look in Shontay's eyes. She tossed her head to get it out of their way, relishing the glow that was now clearly visible in Shontay's pale, burning eyes, the unmistakable lingering heat of a stupendous sexual explosion. Shontay might still hate her, but she would remember this fuck for a long time.

"Still hate me?" Laura whispered, daring her to lie.

Shontay could not suppress a small, involuntary grin as it crossed her delicious, sensual lips, which Laura felt like assaulting again, this instant.

"Yes."

"Even after that?"

"I didn't want it."

"You loved it."

The sly, helpless little grin again. "I . . . couldn't help it."

Slowly, Laura rolled to the side, feeling she might be too heavy since she had been lying on top of Shontay for quite a while now. Shontay actually grabbed her hips and her lower back to keep her from moving.

"No . . . stay there."

"Really?"

Shontay nodded slowly, solemnly. "I like the way it feels with you on top of me."

"In that case, I will never move."

Laura kissed her. This time, Shontay, as if she were a different person, yielded completely to Laura's mouth, and her tongue, raising her hands and lightly caressing Laura's naked back through a long, expressive, emotional kiss. When it was over, she gazed dreamily up into Laura's eyes, trailing one forefinger along Laura's cheek.

"I guess this is the second time you raped me, right?"

Laura gave her a long face. "How could you say such a thing? I couldn't help myself either." She lowered her voice to a sexy growl. "Because I know how hot you are. You make my blood sizzle."

"You are such a fucking liar, Laura."

Laura plunged boldly forward. "I only came up here to ask you down to dinner."

Shontay cocked one eyebrow, maliciously. "What are you serving, black cunt? It's all you like to eat, isn't it?"

Again, Laura moved to get off Shontay's body, but Shontay again held her hips to keep her there. Her eyes, so light brown and mysterious and lovely, bored up into Laura's.

"Don't move. It still feels good."

"You insulted me," Laura pouted.

Shontay's eyes became suddenly dreamy again. "You pulled my hair. God, I came hard. I never knew that would happen."

Laura leaned forward and kissed the blood bruise she had raised on Shontay's lovely neck, which Shontay, of course, did not yet know was there. "If you come downstairs with me," Laura murmured, "I can guarantee one of us is going to eat some black cunt at least."

Shontay broke into a smile. "Now you know why I tried to keep you out. Once I let you in, it's just rape rape rape."

Laura smiled back. "And fuck fuck fuck. Right?"

"I never knew I was this kind of person."

"And what `kind of person' would that be?"

"I don't know . . . sex fiend?"

"Can I take that as an answer to my invitation?"

Shontay sat up and Laura obligingly rolled off her. Laura kissed her shoulder.

"Help me clean Willie's litter box, and I'll come down there with you," Shontay whispered. "We probably scared the living shit out of him with all this fighting and screaming." She looked around them in amazement. "On the floor, too. God . . ."

Shontay was right. Laura had not seen Willie the whole time. Apparently, he had high-tailed it for safety when these two screeching harpies had attacked each other and ended up on the floor fucking like two wild animals. Enough to scare the wits out of any calm, domestic feline. Laura was a little sad about it. She liked Willie, and he had always liked her.

Laura inched closer, embracing her so that their upper bodies, still deliciously naked, pressed together. "Are you sorry?"

Shontay shook her head. "I guess not. You are a liar and a bitch, though. Don't think I don't see through you."

"Did you know you're wildly sexy when you're angry?" Laura said, to deflect her bitterness, which was still apparent.

"Quit trying to change the subject," Shontay said, getting to her feet. "And quit staring at me. I feel like an awkward little girl at the doctor's, or something."

She helped Laura up with one hand, but Laura could not take her eyes off Shontay's tall, thin, but still supple and desirable naked body. Shontay's small, swaying breasts were enchanting, her nipples dark caramel-colored and shiny, tongue-tempting.

As she rose to her feet, Laura held onto Shontay's hand for a moment, drawing her close. "I love your body," she said seriously. "I love it. I want it."

They stood staring deeply into each other's eyes for a few seconds, silent, holding each other's gaze. Then Shontay bent to retrieve her clothes, even the ripped up blouse.

"The litter's in the kitchen, under the sink," she said. "Bring it back to the bathroom and I'll empty the box."

In her absence, Laura searched the hardwood floor for her door key, which she found hidden behind an umbrella stand, then quickly slipped back into her clothes before going to fetch the litter.

In Laura's apartment, Shontay was again stiff and withdrawn. I can't believe she's still angry with me after that glorious fuck upstairs, Laura thought. But then she relented. She had no idea what Shontay's mother—surely it had been her mother; not that dignified old cluck of a father, surely he wouldn't dare bring it up—had told her. Mrs. Gibson might have made it pretty lurid.

Since Laura had ripped apart her favorite blouse, and her bra too, Shontay had found one of her mother's housecoats in the closet and put it on before going with Laura down to Laura's apartment. The housecoat—more a kimono, really, of yellow silk with a pattern of large flamingo-colored flowers on it—made Shontay look both a little dowdy and wildly fetching at the same time. How that could be, Laura didn't know, but just watching her move around with this thin silk thing veiling her long, angular, bony body made Laura wet and hungry for her all over again.

The yellow of the silk was especially alluring against the smooth dark-honey glow of Shontay's marvelous skin.

"I lied," Laura said to her as she fastened the door locks. "I really wasn't fixing dinner. I just wanted to get you down here."

Again the faint, sly little grin that had passed over Shontay's lips earlier returned. "See, I told you you were a fucking liar," she said without, however, smiling more broadly.

Laura stepped closer, lowering her voice, and her eyelids. "I want to take off this kimono thing and kiss you everywhere," she breathed.

Shontay remained coy. "I kind of liked it when you ripped my clothes off. It made me realize you really wanted me."

Laura ran a fingertip across the silk collar of the kimono, then let it slip over the edge onto Shontay's skin. Then she slipped the finger under the silk.

"We shouldn't harm your mother's kimono. She might get suspicious."

But she realized that Shontay was not looking at her but over her shoulder. There was a long oval hallway mirror next to Laura's door, which she often used for a brief check before dashing out. Shontay was squinting into the mirror, her face suddenly reflecting her horror as she raised her hand to her neck, which Laura was about to kiss again, for the umpteenth time.

For a second, Laura thought Shontay was going to strike her again, with the back of her hand. Her face, when screwed up like this in sudden anger, was ferocious and completely scary, as if a mad, slashing fury were about to pour forth.

"Oh god . . . you gave me a hickey!" Shontay wailed, her voice keening upward as she touched the bruise on her beautiful neck with two fingertips, gingerly.

She almost shoved Laura out of the way in her haste to get closer to the mirror. She examined it with intense interest.

"I . . . didn't mean to," Laura stammered awkwardly.

Now Shontay was leaning even closer to the mirror, framing a large portion of her exquisite long neck with the fingers of both hands, tilting her head to the side. Laura found her neck breath-taking anyway and had in truth given her the hickey in a wild, irresistible paroxysm of scorching lust. Looking at it, as Shontay exposed the beautiful expanse of skin to the mirror so she could get a closer look herself, Laura was almost overcome by a fresh wave of the same lust. Somehow, the uneven, purplish blotch on Shontay's perfect light brown skin was exquisitely erotic to her.

She put a hand on Shontay's shoulder, half afraid it would be shrugged off violently. But they had apparently moved beyond the fighting stage, and Shontay was not tense as she turned her face to Laura. All the quick fury had drained out of it, and she was soft and sexy, her eyes alluring, flashing with invitations.

"Nobody ever gave me a hickey before," she said in a hushed voice. "Not that I like it, you cunt. How am I going to cover this up?"

"Mmmm, I could kiss it . . . maybe it'll go away," Laura purred, lifting one swatch of Shontay's hair and nibbling her earlobe.

Shontay giggled, finding this ticklish. "You'll only make it worse."

Laura's lips reached her neck, but she veered away from the hickey, still lifting Shontay's hair, kissing the back of her neck, pulling down the kimono a little to kiss the nape of her neck.

"I could give you a matching one on the other side," she teased.

Shontay shivered, a sharp tremor. "God, you're getting me all excited again."

"Oh good. Come with me." Laura took her hand. "Or did you want me to fix dinner first?"

Shontay smiled, for the first time a warm, girlish, happy, sexual smile. "No. Later."

In Laura's bed, this time there was no struggle, no anger, just slow and devastatingly thorough sensuality. Laura was surprised by the transformation that came over Shontay, who seemed to have received a fresh charge of nasty lechery by the realization that Laura had, unbeknownst to her until now, given her a hickey while fighting and fucking with her on the floor upstairs. She swarmed over Laura, never giving Laura a chance to get the upper hand, which was usual for them, since Shontay was usually the receiver more than the giver.

"Let me, you know, do you in the ass . . . like you do me once in a while," she breathed hotly in Laura's ear. "You always get to have all the fun. Let me stick my finger up your ass and make you scream."

This was enough to make flames leap up happily inside Laura's body. "Are you sure you want to?" Never in the past had Shontay showed any desire to be 'creative.'

Shontay was kissing Laura's neck passionately and replied only by nipping Laura's earlobe. "You are such a bitch . . . I want to make you scream," she murmured sexily. "I want to give you a hickey too."

"Oh god . . . I think you're doing it!" Laura squirmed, feeling hot fire squirt through her pussy as Shontay sucked her neck. "Here . . . honey . . . unhhhhh! Oh! God, that feels good! Here, I'll get the oil for you."

Shontay moderated her love attack long enough for Laura to lean across the bed to the bedside table and open the drawer. She handed the small bottle of baby oil to Shontay, and their eyes locked, throbbing, expectant.

"Do you want a towel?"

Shontay shook her head, her eyes not releasing Laura's. Her stiffish, mussed hair swished around her ears and her neck, making her wildly sexy to Laura. I would let her do anything to me right now, Laura thought. She's so . . . intense. I think she's still really angry at me, but she is full of fuck hunger right now.

For all her usual reserve, Shontay was at the moment apparently overcome by sheer sexual need. Laura was right. As she lay back, Shontay was suddenly all over her again, kissing and stroking her body more aggressively than she had ever done, sucking Laura's nipples hungrily for the first time that night. Still clutching the small plastic bottle, which Laura could feel against her bare skin as Shontay moved over her squirming body, kissing and stroking and sucking it as she descended toward Laura's groin, she finally slid down between Laura's yawning thighs.

"Oh!" Laura gasped as she felt Shontay's lips against her pussy for the first time in weeks.

In keeping with her present mood, Shontay did not waste her time on tenderness or subtlety. Whether it was her desire for Laura or her residual anger from the fight they had had upstairs, she was rough and hungry, spreading Laura's cunt lips with her thumbs and slurping Laura's hot, achy slit passionately. Laura, though hotly aroused, had come quickly and explosively upstairs and was in little danger of coming again too quickly.

Instead, during the next few minutes, she enjoyed and endured a flurry of passion from Shontay that was as startling as it was thrilling. Shontay licked and fingered her cunt rapidly, hungrily, sucking Laura's clit, sliding her fingers between Laura's buns, doing everything to Laura that she had felt Laura do to her in the past. Laura nearly fainted with pleasure, writhing, panting, whimpering as she felt Shontay turn up the heat even further.

"Mmmm, you like that, don't you, you nasty white girl," Shontay grinned up at her, twisting her fingers inside of Laura's pussy, making Laura groan with sexual excitement.

"Unngghhhh! Oh! Aunngghh! Yes . . . yes, honey, do it! Oh Jesus, that feels good!"

"You want me to fuck your little white ass, don't you?" Shontay panted, eyes flaring.

It was so bizarre, Laura realized in the back of her mind. Of all her lovers, Shontay was among the most sophisticated and reserved: regal, college-educated, two professors for parents, in upper management herself, refined, self-controlled, well-mannered. Yet in her lust and anger, she had degenerated into these flagrant racial taunts and insults, which somehow pleased her. She's getting back at me for hurting her, Laura realized. And Laura was a little intimidated by it, but at the same time loved the fierceness that Shontay was showing. They had never had any rough sex together until this evening, but Laura was quickly becoming aware that it wasn't over yet.

There was a brief pause in the onslaught while Shontay fumbled with the snap-open top of the bottle. Laura, lying flat on her back with her thighs spread, feeling ready to be roughly ravished by this fierce beautiful girl who had no idea of her own stark, almost aristocratic appeal, watched in fascination as Shontay spread baby oil all over one long, thin finger. In the middle of lubricating her finger, Shontay's eyes flashed at her.

"You want it?"

Laura nodded. "I want you to do everything to me."

Shontay smiled ambiguously and snapped shut the bottle, leaning across Laura to place it on the bed stand, her small, exquisite breasts swaying delightfully. Laura reached up to touch them, gently scissoring Shontay's nipples in her fingers.

"Let me suck you."

"No." Shontay shook her head, frowning. "I've got something I'm doing."

"Do you know how beautiful you are?"

Shontay grinned. "Quit trying to change the subject."

With a raised eyebrow, she slithered down between Laura's thighs again. Laura felt Shontay's other hand pulling open her ass cheeks, then felt Shontay's greasy fingertip press against her asshole, then felt the long digit slide up into her so deep that it felt twice as long as she knew it was.

"Unnhhh!" she gasped, water coming to her eyes. "Oh . . . yes!"

Shontay grinned up at her, twisting her finger, watching Laura's face. "You like that?"

"Oh yes!"

"How do you like this?"

She began to fuck Laura's asshole very fast with her finger, plunging it in deep, giving Laura short rabbit jabs with it, biting her lower lip in concentration at the same time. Laura was slightly afraid of the glint in Shontay's pale brown eyes, but she was also very aroused by this sharp, thrusting attack. And now Shontay bent her mouth to Laura's pussy too, tonguing and sucking the inflamed cunt lips, taking Laura's throbbing clit into her mouth as her long finger continued to pierce Laura's anus in quick jabs.

"Oh god . . . oh god!" Laura heard herself whimpering, twisting her body, looking down at the maniacal smile on Shontay's face, feeling the sweet pressure of a sexual storm begin to swell in her flesh.

Oh god, I think I might come sooner than I thought, she realized, feeling overwhelmed by Shontay's aggressive hunger. Shontay was fucking her furiously, but the fury and passion seemed to grow out of a confused mixture of desire for Laura's body and hot anger at her at the same time. Then, completely unexpectedly, Shontay, still leaving her finger buried in Laura's clenching ass, slid up to kiss her.

Her torso and her arms were so long that she could do this with relative ease, and as they coiled their tongues together, panting and mewling, she kept fucking Laura's ass slowly and relentlessly with her finger. At the same time, she rubbed her forearm above the wrist into the sopping-wet crease of Laura's swollen pussy, pushing it hard into Laura's splayed cunt, mashing it against Laura's clit, then furiously jabbing Laura's asshole again with her long finger.

"Unhhh! Ohnnn! Ungghhh!" Laura grunted softly, her eyes rolling up, nearly losing it until she felt Shontay's mouth again on her own, tearing savagely at her lips, Shontay's strong, probing tongue nearly sliding down her throat. "Oh shit! Unh! Yes! Oh god . . . Shontay . . . ungghhh!"

"You are such a bitch!" Shontay hissed into Laura's teeth, but without the slightest sign of anger on her face. "I want you to come so hard. So hard . . . like you make me come. I want you to just die when you come."

"I . . . think you're going to get your wish," Laura gasped, now undulating, pushing her ass down into the upward thrusts of Shontay's hand, feeling her flesh pulse and throb with the first hints of an arriving orgasm.

Shontay was a whirlwind. Laura had never seen her like this, a hot tornado, cradling Laura's shoulders in her arms and fucking Laura's ass furiously with her other hand, mashing her forearm into Laura's pussy, kissing and sucking Laura's neck, then dropping her mouth to Laura's breasts, tearing at her nipples, before moving her head up again to see the contortions of intense pleasure and near-desperation on Laura's face.

Laura's hands fluttered up spasmodically, trying to clutch Shontay's body, trying to caress her and embrace her, but she was quickly overcome by the intensity and sharp passion of Shontay's fuck-assault. She could feel her fingertips brush Shontay's erect nipples, even feel the firm, smooth flesh of her small breasts, and the ripple of her ribcage, the wave-like up and down motion of her hard stomach as she breathed rapidly. But she could not get a grip on the girl's squirming body anywhere, and soon her own body was engulfed by spasms so acute that it became pointless anyway.

"Auungghhh!" Laura cried out, her body suddenly arching of its own accord into the air, almost levitating off the mattress.

As Laura collapsed back to the bed, Shontay gave her a crushing embrace, so fierce that she wondered where the girl's strength had come from. Shontay was now half on top of her, still fucking her furiously, and whimpering and gasping too with incredible sexual excitement. Laura felt a pulverizing bolt of hot coming rip through her, nearly knocking her breath out.

"Unngghhh!"

"Oh yes . . . oh Laura yes!" Shontay gasped, as her hand stopped thrusting and she held Laura in a death grip.

"Auungghh!" Laura finally cried out again as her breath returned. "Mnnngghiiieeeee! Ohnnnnggg! Mnnngghiiieeeee!"

A ferocious climax wrenched her. She shuddered violently, undulating in long, involuntary waves as a stream of wracking spasms poured through her shaking body. For a brief few seconds, she became unaware of anything else, unaware of Shontay holding her, of Shontay's finger thrust up her ass, of Shontay's hard, bony forearm mashed into her throbbing cunt. Only the white-hot wrenching spasms of her orgasm filled her consciousness, until they began to grow less strong, less frequent, and she drifted back to awareness to find herself still in Shontay's death grip.

After a few seconds, even though Laura was thrilled to be held so tightly, it began to hurt.

"Could you . . . let me go for a minute?" she panted, looking up almost worshipfully into Shontay's warm, pale brown eyes, now soft with sexual caring. "I . . . can't breathe."

Shontay smiled and released her grip. "Sorry. I got carried away. I never made you, or anybody, come like that."

"Not me, at least," Laura gulped, slowly rubbing her arms where Shontay had clasped them so fiercely.

Now Shontay was totally serious and concerned, her solicitude so far removed from her earlier sexual rage and mania that at first Laura had trouble getting used to it.

Shontay, in contrast to being stiff with anger and spite, was soft and pliant, warm and affectionate, stroking Laura's shoulder, cupping Laura's breast, her lips parted and inviting. Laura leaned up and kissed her, at the same time looping one arm behind Shontay's neck and drawing her down to the bed again.

They kissed very sweetly for about a minute, Laura's hand crawling up to Shontay's small, wonderful breasts and squeezing them suggestively.

"I hope you know you aren't getting away with that," she whispered when their lips came apart.

Shontay grinned, almost bashfully. "You mean you're going to pay me back?"

"What do you think?" Laura said, rolling her onto her back. "I'm going to give you a matching hickey on the other side."

Shontay suddenly winced in fear. "Oh . . . please don't! One is enough. God, I'll have to hide it with makeup or something."

Laura snuggled up to her, kissing her under the chin, nipping her ear. "If I don't, will you let me lick that beautiful little pussy of yours? I've been dying to all night."

Shontay nodded. "I will . . . let you."

Laura smiled and kissed her cheek, then her neck again, right on the plum-colored splotch of the hickey she had given her. "I promise to make it up to you for this," she whispered.

Laura loved Shontay's body. Though it was long and thin, a little bony and angular in places, you would never know that under her clothes, Shontay had this high, round, pert little ass, so beautifully hard and shapely, or these exquisite small breasts. Her skin also, this richly amber, light molasses skin was impossibly, thrillingly smooth under Laura's lips and her fingertips as she drifted down the girl's incredibly long stomach and belly, pausing frequently to kiss and nuzzle Shontay's delightfully perfect flesh. Anybody who doesn't want to fuck this delicious girl every day is crazy, she thought.

Because they had been fighting, Laura had not yet had a chance to kiss and stroke this marvelous flesh, and now that Shontay had finally yielded to her, apparently having released much of her anger and feelings of rejection for the moment, Laura could indulge her desire to the fullest. She began by descending slowly, kissing the velvety skin of

Shontay's taut midriff, letting her lips skim the light, invisible down that rose in infinitesimal soft filaments from it, then pausing at Shontay's deep navel to toy briefly with her in this sensitive region.

But instead of continuing down, she let her lips and hands travel up again to Shontay's lovely small breasts, now kissing and tonguing

Shontay's dark caramel nipples tenderly, lovingly, until she heard Shontay beginning to moan softly, and saw her twisting, biting her lip.

"Ohhnnnn! Oh . . . Laura . . . oh god it feels good!"

It felt marvelous to Laura. While she was kissing and sucking Shontay's small, firm breasts, she slid her hands down the girl's long naked back to her hard little buns, cupping one in each palm and digging her fingers into the resilient flesh, about the size of two round grapefruits. She squeezed them and sucked harder on one of Shontay's nipples.

"Ohhhh . . . I love your body," she breathed, moving her mouth over to the other one, sliding one long forefinger up and down the warm, moist crack between Shontay's hard little buns.

"Oh! Oh yes!" Shontay panted, gently but urgently pushing down on Laura's shoulders with her hands, now writhing more uncontrollably. "Oh yes, Laura . . . I need it . . . oh yes . . . I want it."

Now Laura did slide down, down, further, sliding between Shontay's thighs. "I want to taste this pretty pussy so much," she purred to Shontay, spreading the silky jet-black filaments of hair away from the wet, puckered little love chute.

She had tasted it often before but rarely got enough. Even though Shontay's lovely long naked body was a delicious light molasses hue, her small, gaping cunt lips were black as night, and now oily and shiny with flowing nectars, very wet and tongue-tempting. Between the parted inner lips was a squinchy wet pink feast of raw flesh, and Laura immediately slipped her tongue right into the center of it.

"Anngghh!" Shontay groaned, her body stiffening almost immediately, her long, smooth thigh muscles clenching.

Again Laura got her hands on the girl's lovely curved ass, sliding both of them under Shontay's clenching buns and squeezing them again a she tongued and sucked Shontay's wet black cunt lips, then again burrowed her tongue deep into the juicy pink flesh inside them. Shontay, even with Laura's considerable skill and assistance, often did not come quickly, but this time she was apparently on fire. She began keening and whimpering deep in her throat, then actually thrashed around violently on her back as Laura turned up the heat, flogging Shontay's clit with her tongue, sucking it, and roughly squeezing Shontay's ass cheeks at the same time. She pushed her mouth hungrily into Shontay's streaming cunt, mouth-raping it savagely.

"Oh! Oh!" Shontay whimpered. "Oh god! Laura . . . please! Like I did you. Please!"

Laura quickly realized that Shontay wanted the same thing she had given Laura. They had never really got into some of the more devious sexual practices Laura shared with some other girls, but early in their relationship, Laura had given Shontay a piercing, electrifying orgasm by inserting one long forefinger up into her ass just as she was beginning to come, and Shontay had never forgotten it.

"Oh yes . . . baby . . . you can have anything you want," she murmured to Shontay, glancing over at the bed stand, where Shontay had deposited the small magic bottle.

It took her a little quick maneuvering, but in a few seconds, she had it open and spread a little oil on her finger. Then she snapped it back shut, and pushed it down on the bed near her feet, not bothering to take the time to lean back over Shontay's long, jerking legs to reach the table.

"Oh yes . . . hold on, honey, here it comes," she purred, again licking the dewy black petals of Shontay's delicious slit and slithering her tongue between them, while at the same time parting the girl's hard little buns with the fingers of her left hand.

"Ungghhh!" Shontay groaned, her body suddenly leaping in a violent twitch as she felt Laura's long greased forefinger sliding up into her ass. "Oh . . . god!"

"Yes . . ." Laura purred. "Yes . . . yes . . . go for it, honey . . ."

"Oh! Unh! Unh! Oh shit! Oh yes . . . unhhhhhh!"

Now Laura, knowing Shontay was right on the edge, ready to fall over, unleashed all of her passion. Skewering Shontay's ass on her twisting finger, she again assaulted the girl's sweet, festering pussy with her mouth, sucking Shontay's clit sharply, fucking her ass fervently, feeling Shontay's long, stiffening body suddenly shudder in a deep rumble of release.

"Auungghhh!" Shontay roared, flexing so hard that her long, supple body made a huge, awkward flip off the bed, then fell back into it, writhing and squealing as shattering spasms of coming wrenched her. "Iiiiieeeeennnggghhh! Ungghiiieeeee!" she yelped, again flipping, surging off the mattress, jamming her ass down into Laura's finger, grinding her pussy into Laura's mouth as each succeeding shockwave struck her.

Laura held on. With her free arm looped around one of Shontay's slender, silky thighs, she rocked up and down with Shontay's wild gyrations until they slowly began to weaken, and Shontay's rough, labored breathing became more audible than her wild screams. When her pelvic girdle finally came to rest, Laura could still feel distant rhythmic contractions going on deep inside Shontay's body somewhere. Shontay's soft, sensitive mewling seemed to grow out of the deep hum of ecstasy that still flowed through her slackening body.

"Oh god," she said, half whimpering while looking down at Laura, her face reflecting the stunned feeling that clearly pervaded her flesh. "I think that was the best ever."

Laura was very careful in slowly extracting her finger, watching intense sensations centered in her plundered rectum replace the stunned look on Shontay's face. "Even better than the one upstairs?" she asked softly, smiling.

Now that Laura's finger was completely out, Shontay recovered her composure. She sat up, smiling back sheepishly. "I liked them both."

"Me too. Now, how about that dinner I promised you."

"Do you mind if we just . . . I don't know, snuggle a little first?"

Shontay was very soft and shy and somber, and Laura could not in any way violate this mood. The girl seemed almost sad, more deeply pensive than Laura had ever seen her. Laura's Latin was not strong, but she had taken a course in high school. *Post coitum omne animal triste est.* All animals are sad after fucking, she translated to herself.

In fact, she felt a little sad herself, probably because of the fight, first, and then the sweet fucking here in her bed, the clear and simple determination they both had to please the other. Why should that make me sad? She wondered. I guess because she is seeing it as the change our relationship will now reflect, that this seals it. I sleep with others too, and she will have to bear the hurt.

"I would love to snuggle," Laura whispered, stretching out next to her.

They held one another without speaking for a long time.

"You smell so good," Laura finally broke the silence, burrowing her nose in Shontay's hair.

"You say that to all the girls," Shontay said, but not in a kidding tone.

Laura thought of Sara. True, she had said it to Sara. It was true, too. They both smelled wonderful to her. And very different, for some reason.

"If I keep smelling you, I'm going to want you again," Laura said, ignoring Shontay's comment. "Smelling you makes my pussy get a little buzzy feeling deep inside. You know that?" She ran her fingertip over Shontay's sensual lips before kissing them again. "I'm sorry about your favorite blouse. And that beautiful bra. I hope you'll let me replace them."

Shontay put her own fingertip on Laura's lower lip. "I'm glad you want me, Laura. Nobody ever wanted me the way you do. Nobody ever wanted me enough to rape me, and you've already done it twice." Her eyes were big and round and pale brown, so unusual and hypnotic.

"I can't believe that," Laura whispered, kissing the fingertip warmly, unable to suppress the beginnings of a blush. "You're making me feel guilty. Come on in and help me cook. We're going to wear each other out without some sustenance."

"Why don't we take a bath together instead?" Shontay said, suddenly bright and cheerful, as if the idea had just occurred to her.

"No wonder you're so skinny," Laura teased, poking her in her delectable ribs, wanting to kiss them all over again, and the rest of this long, smooth, light brown body too. "You turn down food at every opportunity."

Shontay's eyes flashed. "I thought you liked my skinny body."

Laura tilted her head. "Compromise, okay? We eat . . . then we bathe . . . and . . . whatever. You're going to wear me out, girl. Didn't you hear me?"

"What's the matter, Laura, getting old?" Shontay said, with an ambiguous wink.

<<O>>

But Shontay had, a few weeks later, due to simple bad luck for Laura, caught Laura leaving her own apartment with Taneesha, Deshona's stunning young niece, in tow, after having fucked the darling girl nearly to shreds all afternoon. Laura knew they both reeked of lascivious bed games. It had been, to put it mildly, an awkward moment. Though she and Shontay had no claims on one another, Laura knew after the intimacy they had shared—a horrific catfight followed by a scorching sexual makeup—that Shontay felt a deep physical awakening caused by Laura and now violated by Laura's clearly randy and ungovernable promiscuity.

From that moment on, Shontay spurned Laura with an icy scorn that made Laura tremble to think that anyone you had shared piercing orgasms with could be so cold. Shontay by now would not even speak to her. She would only scowl at her coldly if their paths crossed at work, sometimes even moving to the other side of the corridor in an aloof and frigid manner, to show that Laura was leprous and untouchable. Her hair was yanked and knotted back behind her head more severely than ever, and she walked stiffly and with military precision, head held high imperiously on her delicious long neck.

Laura, pausing in amazement and mild sorrow at these withering rejections, found herself wondering if she would be craving the girl's body so much if she didn't know what lay underneath those awkward, baggy, even aggressively ugly business suits Shontay wore, having reverted to them after wearing for a while thin, summery dresses that showed off her marvelous café-au-lait skin and long, slender, but thrilling legs. The transformation was simply a return to her previous self, her pre-Laura self, as if all that hot sex and blossoming confidence in her physical appeal had never happened.

Laura also wondered in passing if she didn't feel the fires ignite in her pussy when Shontay marched so stiffly and contemptuously by her because that kind of scornful rejection only fanned the flames of her lust and doubled her determination to break through it. She had done it before in spite of, it seemed, impossible odds.

Since falling hard for Sara, and then getting involved, lamentably, with Dee Dee, Laura had seen less and less of Shontay, and Shontay, being fiercely bright and perceptive, had quickly picked up on Laura's shifting alliances. Even Laura's grief over losing Sara, it was obviously clear to Shontay, did not involve her. Laura wasn't moping because they hadn't slept together for a week. She was instead mooning after some rival, which sent Shontay not into the dumps but into a purple fury that she could barely contain.

Her manner, however, was not to protest or whine or accuse. Instead, she withdrew into an icy contempt, implacable and frosty. As Laura had often reflected in the past, it was Shontay's 'Off with her head!' manner.

Since they worked in totally different spheres of the business, their paths rarely crossed. Occasionally, however, their presence was required at all-management meetings, and during one of stupefying dullness that had been called to review company financial goals, Laura found herself in a good position to gaze at Shontay for about forty-five minutes. Sitting behind a couple of men with broad shoulders, Laura was half-concealed and could admire Shontay unobtrusively, without seeming to stare; just a causal glance now and then.

Shontay was every bit the ice queen that her reputation called for, her head held high, her gaze sharp and imperious, her scowl intimidating. She was also ostentatiously taking notes, scribbling stiffly and conscientiously on a yellow pad in her lap.

Today she wore the off-white, ivory version of her baggy business suit, which hung on her bony frame like ill-cut draperies, the expensive fabric contrasting wildly with the awkward folds and ripples. The contrast of the ivory fabric with her skin, though, was ravishing. After days of rhapsodizing over the sleek, deeply black skin of Charise and Dee Dee, Laura was mildly startled to recall how enchanting she always found the rich pale clover honey hues of Shontay's skin, so richly highlighted by the ivory fabric of her suit jacket.

Her long swan's neck was delectably visible, even more so with her hair bundled up so tightly behind her head, and the shape of her jaw and her exquisite brown ears were just as perfect as they could be. She was really quite lovely, if you knew her as Laura did (naked, Laura thought, cursing herself for this salacious aside), and it was a great mystery why she felt compelled to appear so reserved, crisp, and scornfully distant. While watching her, Laura recalled how once, when they were lying together in bed after vigorously fucking, Shontay had confessed that though she usually seemed very much in control, she was actually 'scared shitless' most of the time.

Laura wondered if she were scared shitless at this moment. Probably not, she realized. Safety in numbers. Shontay, as if she could feel Laura staring, finally toward the end of the meeting whipped her head around nervously. Laura, safe behind her screen formed by the two men in front of her, merely leaned down to adjust her shoe, and successfully evaded this scrutiny.

She did manage deliberately to run into Shontay at the exit of the meeting room, slyly stepping in front of her to prevent her smooth escape.

"Oh . . . hi!" Laura said brightly, gazing up into those mysterious pale brown eyes that always had a hypnotic effect on her. "Long time no see."

Shontay was nearly four inches taller than Laura and could make anyone blanch by staring down from such a height. She scowled and looked like she wanted to flee. Finally, a pinched, noncommittal smile crossed her lips.

"Hello, Laura." She glowered, her light brown eyes flecked with sparks of anger, as if to accuse Laura of blocking her way, which was true.

"I . . . miss . . . our talks," Laura smiled, trying to appear as friendly as possible. Shontay had accused her often of only wanting 'black cunt,' her way of saying Laura was only after her sweet little pussy. And even though Shontay had exquisite skin the rich color of light molasses, her pussy was indeed very black, Laura knew—the lips, at least.

Oh god, Laura thought, Dee Dee had said the same thing. Maybe I'm becoming too obvious, too crude.

Shontay pursed her lips. "Right. See you, Laura."

She slipped around Laura and stalked down the hallway, not looking back. Fortunately, most of the meeting attendees had dispersed by this time, so that no one was nearby to notice this snub. Good thing, Laura reflected. Company headquarters staff were like the inhabitants of a small village when it came to gossip. She watched Shontay disappear, unable to keep her eyes from straying to the woman's marvelous high little rump that yawed and swayed ever so slightly as she walked, that jutted out a little, something not even the loosely hanging swaths of cloth could conceal.

Laura, though temporarily crestfallen, adjusted to this rejection, feeling that Shontay was certainly within her rights. Laura was deeply and painfully in love with Sara still, and whatever attention she could give Shontay would certainly not be what Shontay appeared to require of her.

To take her mind off it, she slept with Shavon a couple of times, and once with Yvette, always such intense experiences that nothing could put them in the shadows. Mercifully, Dee Dee was out of town in Ann Arbor, trying to see if she could get admitted there in the spring to complete her Ph.D. program. (Sara had paid for the trip.) Laura, though still suffering great miseries of rejected love over Sara, had come to a gradual realization that it was probably really over. This made her less reluctant to sleep with Dee Dee, especially since their times together were hot enough to burn up the planet. On the other hand, she could never quite relinquish a belief in the possibility that Sara would come back to her, and then the shit would hit the fan all over again when she found out that Laura had been screwing Dee Dee regularly.

She had absolutely no evidence to back up this belief.

A few days after this meeting in which Laura ogled Shontay from three rows away, and got contemptuously snubbed at the exit door, an obligatory management retreat was announced. It would be held at a resort in Santa Cruz that was especially designed for business meetings, and would occupy three days of the following week.

Being currently unencumbered by relationships, Laura enjoyed driving down alone, trying not to think of Sara, or what unknown faculty members, male or female, Dee Dee might be fucking in Ann Arbor in order to grease the wheels of graduate admissions. I really became wound up with these two beautiful women, didn't I? She realized.

She hummed to herself, her old standby.

I fall in love too easily,
I fall in love too fast,
I fall in love too terribly hard,
For love to ever last . . .

After a while her thoughts deviated to Shontay, whom she knew would also be at this retreat. Oh god, another three days of freezing stares and huffy tossing of the head. Looking at that long smooth neck . . . that pretty little rump. Those hypnotic light brown eyes. Can I stand it? Having her wither me with a glance?

Forcibly, almost as if to get her mind off Shontay and the mixed blessing it would be to be thrown together with her at this retreat, she let her mind drift back to Sara. Now that she was (mostly) convinced they would never be together again, she could indulge her pained and elaborate fantasies to the fullest, imagining what it would be like at this very instant to be pressing her lips to the swollen, dewy black petals of Sara's lovely wet pussy, nuzzling with her nose the silvery pussy ring, letting the tip of her tongue find the little firm nub of clit underneath it, hearing Sara gasp.

This fantasy almost made Laura's heart stop, before filling again with a sharp pain of loss, and she had to tighten her grip on the wheel in order not to veer off the road. I better think of something else.

I guess I'll have to dream the rest . . . she hummed again.
If you can't remember the things that we said,
Those nights when my shoulder held your sleepy head,
If you believe that parting's best,
I guess I'll have to dream the rest . . .

At the resort, she got settled in her room and went out to the pool. There would be a group dinner, preceded by a cocktail party, but until then her time was her own. She knew Shontay would not be appearing at the pool—even if she had already arrived—because she was very self-conscious about her 'skinny' figure. Laura, on the other hand, had nothing to hide and even enjoyed the stares she frequently drew. Let them want, let them wonder, she thought, realizing that she sounded a lot like Dee Dee.

After dinner on the second night (the first had passed without incident, and she had only rarely glimpsed Shontay at the party and the dinner), Laura found herself with about five other management employees in the room of the French representative of their company, playing *Trivial Pursuit*. It was a friendly and uproarious game, and she enjoyed herself immensely. On her way back to her room, she stopped by the small lobby shop for a magazine and ran directly into Shontay, who was clutching an issue of *Marie Claire* in her hand and heading for the counter.

"Oh . . . hi," Shontay said, caught by surprise.

"Hi, Shontay," Laura said calmly. She began leafing through a magazine, more as a prop than anything else, just to be doing something, not looking directly at Shontay.

Shontay continued to the counter and paid for her magazine. Laura was right behind her as she left the shop. Shontay looked around.

"I wish we could talk," Laura said softly, though as far as she could tell only resort employees were left in the lobby.

Shontay looked tired and a little distracted. No wonder, Laura thought. Trying to keep up that cold, hostile exterior all day, all the time. Must be a real effort.

"I don't think we have anything to talk about, Laura."

Laura pursed her lips. "Come on, I'll buy you a drink." She pointed with her head toward the bar.

"You know I don't drink. Hardly ever."

Laura smirked at her, teasingly. "This is a retreat. Make an exception. We're supposed to relax. Get to know each other."

"I already know you as well as I want to," Shontay said, her voice cutting, her face sour.

"Ouch." Laura winced visibly. "You're so cold."

Shontay's pale light brown eyes clouded over briefly, as if this conversation were causing her as much distress as it was causing Laura. "I'm tired. I'm going to my room. Good night, Laura."

Not knowing what else to do, Laura watched her walk away, her magazine clutched in a thick roll under one arm. "By the way, how's Willie?" she half-shouted after Shontay, surprised at the way her voice reverberated through the mostly deserted lobby.

It was a little embarrassing, but a quick look around told her that no one had heard. Shontay turned and appeared shocked that anyone would holler at her after her withering comments. She frowned, as if Laura were an unpredictable maniac. Willie was her parents' cat. Her parents had lived in the apartment above Laura's, until Laura had recently moved.

"I . . . miss him," Laura stammered. "Willie and I . . . always got along."

"Willie's fine," Shontay said coldly.

But this mere pause allowed Laura to cross the space between them again. Now she spoke more softly, intimately.

"If you won't have a drink, why don't we sit by the pool for a few minutes? I really would like to talk to you."

"We have nothing to talk about."

Laura let her gaze fall from Shontay's mesmerizing eyes to her sensual lips. If simple civility would not work, she was willing to try veiled sexual invitation. She realized that sex was really the root cause of Shontay's hostility, and yet they had shared so many intense sexual moments, and sweet ones too, that Laura wondered how Shontay could ignore them.

"I just like to be near you," Laura whispered. "Just for a few minutes?"

Shontay shook her head. She turned and began walking away again. This time Laura followed. They reached the place where the wings of the convention center forked, leading to two different corridors of rooms. Laura stopped and watched Shontay go down one. Shontay looked over her shoulder and saw Laura watching her. She came back.

"Are you following me?" Her eyes looked amused as well as angry.

"I . . . I'm sorry," Laura looked down.

There was a long, painful silence. Laura could hear Shontay breathing.

"Hell . . . if you want to talk so much, okay," Shontay finally said. She began walking back in the same direction, toward her room. "Don't you know we shouldn't be seen having a quarrel like this? Somebody might see us and think we're . . . you know, closer than we are."

Laura followed her without a word. Why is she doing this, she wondered. Why is she inviting me in, after being so cold and mean? Shontay opened the door with her key but paused, turning to Laura.

"Only for a few minutes. Nothing's happening."

"I know. I promise. Just a few minutes."

After turning on the bright overhead light to completely illuminate the darkened room, Shontay turned on the small, dimmer light by the bed, then switched off the first one. She tossed her magazine on the bed and sat down next to it, since there was only one chair. Laura sat in it.

Shontay's face was blank, expressionless. She almost glowered at Laura, waiting for her to begin.

"You wanted to talk."

Laura squirmed. She clasped her hands and rubbed them together awkwardly. "I . . . think I just wanted to be near you. For a few minutes. Without you glowering at me."

Shontay gave Laura one of her patented, pinched smiles. "How's this?"

"I want to kiss you," Laura said, so softly that both of them could barely hear her.

"Laura, you are such a cunt."

"What a thing to say," Laura teased, with a long face. "I made you pant. I made you quiver."

Shontay nodded seriously. "I can do without it."

Laura raised one eyebrow and shrugged. She started to get up. "I can't force you."

"You don't have to go yet," Shontay said, without moving.

Laura sat back. "I don't?"

Shontay shook her head. "Tell me what you think of the meeting."

They discussed the meeting for a few minutes, though Laura was very guarded and noncommittal. Shontay seemed to be fishing, but not too hard. She smoked, opening the window wide to let out the smoke.

"I'm not supposed to smoke in here. It's a non-smoking room."

Laura knew that Shontay smoked when she got nervous. She smoked two cigarettes in a row.

"May I kiss you now?" Laura whispered, getting up from the chair, as Shontay snubbed out the second cigarette.

Shontay seemed paralyzed, her pale brown eyes pulsing as she looked up at Laura coming across the small room. There was no sign on her face of the implacable hostility that earlier had been there. Still, she shook her head. Laura stopped.

"No kissing." She turned her cheek to the side to deflect Laura's kiss, which grazed her cheekbone instead.

Laura pulled back. "Sorry. I thought . . . since we're both forced to be here at this cruddy meeting, we might comfort each other a little."

Shontay gave her a sharp look. "You don't like the meeting? You were lying earlier?"

Laura shrugged. "I never said I liked it."

"I'm on the planning committee for this off-site," Shontay said, sounding wounded. "Tell me what you don't like about it."

"I'd rather not," Laura said, trying to kiss her again.

"Cut it out!" Shontay scooted to the side. "What are you going to do, rape me? Isn't that what you do every time I see you?"

Laura smiled understandingly. "I didn't think you objected. Before."

"I object now. Maybe you'd better go."

"Shontay, you're very lovely. May I take your hair down? You always look so sexy with your hair down. It makes me just . . . quiver inside. Turn your head, and I'll take your hair down for you."

"Don't you touch me!"

Now Laura believed she meant it. Shontay was shaking with fury. Laura backed off. "Okay . . . okay. I know when I'm not wanted."

She pulled back, still standing, not really knowing what to do. Shontay looked completely discombobulated and did not stand up for a few seconds. When she did, she strode in just two steps to the door, her legs being very long and the room very small. Laura looked at her sadly.

But Shontay herself was apologizing as she held the door open for Laura. "I'm sorry . . . it just didn't work out," she mumbled.

Laura paused, half in the door and half out. She whispered, not wanting any stray passerby in the hallway to hear her. "I'm sorry you feel the way you do."

She raised one finger to Shontay's cheek and caressed it, slowly, meaningfully. Then she turned and walked down the dark corridor to the fork, then up the other wing to her own room. She did not know if Shontay was watching her as she walked away, but she did not hear the door shut.

Back in her own room, she showered, then turned on the TV, sound down low, to distract herself. She must have nodded off briefly, for she was awakened by a soft rapping at her door. She crossed the room and opened it a crack, leaving the brass chain fastened.

"Shontay." Quickly, Laura unfastened the chain. "How did you find my room?"

"Are you going to let me in?" Shontay snapped, under her breath.

"Of course."

Laura opened the door, and Shontay slipped inside. Laura's heart had started thumping inside her chest when she noticed that Shontay had taken her hair down. It hung in disheveled clumps around her ears and cheeks. She was wearing a cream-colored terry cloth bathrobe that made her honey-hued skin more beautiful than ever.

"I . . . peeked," Shontay confessed, looking briefly at the floor in embarrassment. "When you left . . . I walked behind you and peeked down the hall. To see which one you went into."

Since Laura did not dare to say anything else at the moment, she closed the door and refastened the chain. Both of them watched her fingers, as if it were a significant gesture, resonating with sexual overtones, the mere slipping of a knob of metal into a slot. Laura turned off the TV. She looked at Shontay, who seemed petrified.

Calm down, honey, Laura said with her eyes, still not daring to speak. We've done this before. Remember?

They were both still standing, only inches apart, since Laura's room was as small as Shontay's. Laura crossed the remaining distance, looking up, since Shontay was so tall.

"Ready for that kiss now?"

Shontay didn't say anything. She didn't move away, either. "I . . . was sorry you left," she whispered. "I'm sorry I made you leave."

"There's nothing for anyone to be sorry about," Laura murmured, uptilting her mouth to Shontay's, trying to beckon Shontay to lower hers a little, since their lips were still inches apart.

"Maybe I should go," Shontay said, suddenly.

This, Laura knew, was a way of acknowledging that if she stayed, they would fuck. Laura smiled at her gently. Shontay was always so skittish, like a thoroughbred.

"I'd be very unhappy if you did," Laura said.

Now Shontay's pale, light brown eyes swam with sexual meanings that she could not suppress. "Okay, then," she said, very softly. "I'm ready."

To make it special, Laura raised both hands to her face, luxuriating in the feel of Shontay's hair brushing her fingers, swinging loose around her cheeks, and pulled Shontay's mouth gently down into hers. A thrilling electric charge coursed through both of them as their lips met, a scintillating current born of their estrangement, the time that had elapsed since they had last done this, and their evasive circling since then.

Shontay's mouth was warm and sensual, and Laura's lips curved into hers slowly, with agonizing sensitivity, before their tongues even met. She was in no hurry and wanted to enjoy every micro-second of this to the fullest. Finally, Shontay's teeth parted, and Laura's tongue slithered inside her mouth, probing, dancing, exploring the entire warm wet cavity, coiling with Shontay's tongue now. She still held Shontay's face in both hands. Shontay was soft and yielding, so different from her earlier sharp, hostile manner. She yielded her mouth to Laura's, letting Laura's tongue fuck her mouth without any counter aggression, until finally the fire inside grew too hot and she began to kiss Laura back more hungrily.

Now Laura was forced into the passive role as Shontay drove her tongue deep into her mouth. Shontay clutched Laura's body through Laura's thin housecoat, and Laura dropped her own hands, finding the sash of Shontay's bathrobe and pulling it loose. She slipped her hands inside, clasping the girl's warm, lean, naked body.

Shontay had a long, supple back that was just a dream of rapture for Laura, who ran her fingers all over it, feeling the long smooth muscles that ran the length of it from her shapely shoulder blades all the way down to her dimpled sacrum.

"I love your back," Laura whispered, momentarily disentangling her tongue from Shontay's, panting. "I want to kiss it all over . . . god, what a beautiful back."

She swept her hands forward as Shontay began kissing her again, pulling them up to Shontay's enchanting small breasts, the size of delicate teacups. Anyone who did not know Shontay's body well, as Laura did, would have been surprised to find them there since in most of her clothes Shontay looked severely flat-chested. But in fact, she had these marvelous, perfect little globes, firm and round, capped by thick, dark caramel nipples that Laura was now pinching gently, insistently.

Shontay pulled back from kissing Laura long enough to smile. "You like those too, don't you?" she panted, her lips wet with Laura's saliva, her eyes shiny and hot.

It had taken her a long time to get to the point where she could enjoy Laura's adoration of her naked body. Shontay was very tall and thin, even skinny, some would say, with thin thighs and marvelously etched bone structure, prominent collarbones, rounded but also slightly bony shoulders. Her ribcage protruded slightly, and her elbows and knees were occasionally a little awkward. But she had a model's body, and certainly a model's face, when she let her hair down, and once you got used to the length of her body and its angles, you could easily become enraptured by it, Laura knew. This rapture of Laura's was almost the sole cause of Shontay's becoming prouder of her physical charms. And ever since that had occurred, she had loved teasing Laura about Laura's hunger for them.

"Tell me how you love my titties," she whispered in Laura's ear, her fingers now scrabbling for the buttons on Laura's housecoat.

"I could eat them for breakfast, lunch and dinner," Laura murmured, pulling open the bathrobe now, squeezing the marvelous small globes. "I could suck them in my sleep."

"Ooooohhhhh," Shontay giggled softly, "you're awake now."

"Oh, I can suck them when I'm awake too."

Laura dropped her mouth to Shontay's breasts, holding them in her hands and peppering them with hot kisses, enchanted by seeing more and more of Shontay's rich honey velvet skin come into view. In the dim light of her room it glowed with a fine sheen like light molasses, and Laura extended her tongue, licking wide swoops around Shontay's glimmering caramel nipples, then letting her lips approach closer to one while Shontay looked down at her mouth.

"Ahhh!" she gasped as Laura sucked the shiny, soft caramel bud inside.

Laura sucked it gently at first, swirling her tongue all around Shontay's nipple and feeling it grow thicker and pulpier inside her wet mouth. Shontay stroked Laura's head, whimpering softly, watching. The harder her nipple became in Laura's mouth, the harder Laura sucked it, until Shontay was moaning and trembling.

"Oh shit . . . I've got to lie down, Laura," she gasped. "You're making my legs weak. God, you do that so well!"

"Quick, lie down on the bed," Laura murmured. "Here, take this off."

Shontay was pliant and obedient, so different from her earlier self, slipping the bathrobe off her body with Laura's help. Laura was quickly out of her housecoat too, and she pulled the bed coverings down, exposing the sheet, in one rapid motion.

"We'll have to be very quiet," she whispered to Shontay, as they stretched out facing one another.

Shontay's pale brown eyes were wide and shiny. She nodded. "I know."

Laura gazed deep into them, hypnotized as usual by their odd sexual power over her. "Now give me that other lovely little breast," she breathed.

Shontay, half-embarrassed but saucy at the same time, cupped her other breast in one hand, looking down, offering it to Laura. "You can do it a little harder, if you want," she murmured.

"Mmmm, does it make your pretty pussy wet when I suck you hard?" Laura asked, quickly taking Shontay's other nipple into her mouth, laving it fervidly with her tongue.

"Oh god, yes!" Shontay whimpered again.

Laura smiled up at her, holding Shontay's wet, erect, caramel nipple playfully between her teeth. She released it momentarily. "Can I see how wet it is?"

The same half-embarrassed but sexually excited grin passed across Shontay's face. She nodded.

But Laura was unwilling to leave Shontay's marvelous small breasts just yet and resumed sucking the wet, pointing nipple she had just released, then returned to the first one, mouth-mauling it passionately now. Shontay squirmed. Her fingers fluttered in Laura's hair, and she arched her back a little, pushing her wet nipples into Laura's face.

"Now . . . let me see," Laura teased softly. "Should I see how wet it is with my finger . . . or my tongue?"

Shontay giggled and panted nervously. "Either one."

"Which do you like the most?"

"Tongue."

"Mmmm . . . it's a long way down this long, beautiful body," Laura purred, now descending, her lips moving skillfully across Shontay's long, palpitating stomach, kissing it everywhere.

"Oh Laura . . ."

Now that she had Shontay in her bed, Laura was in no rush. Though many may have thought Shontay's naked body to be overly angular, bony, and thin, Laura found it enchanting. Shontay's honey-gold skin was covered with a fine, silky down that Laura reveled in rubbing her cheek against, and she could feel the fine silk under her sensitive lips as they inched slowly down the taut, heaving muscles of the girl's very long midriff.

She had to pause for a few seconds at the glistening, raven-black curls of Shontay's small pubic patch of hair, nuzzling the sparkly filaments with her nose, letting the ripe perfumes of Shontay's aroused cunt drift up to her nostrils. She had not tasted this exquisite pussy for weeks, maybe almost two months by now, and she recognized a sharp, sudden hunger in herself for it.

Unlike the rest of her body—long arms, long legs, long torso, long neck, everything very long—Shontay's beautiful pussy was a small treasure, a juicy little wet magenta slot enclosed by glossy black cunt lips that were now gaping and swollen. At the top, presently concealed, was, Laura knew, a tiny but very sensitive clit that she loved to coax out with her tongue, while feeling Shontay's body twinge and clench in fierce anticipation of the climax she often had some difficulty reaching.

"Oh honey," Laura murmured, kissing the smooth, warm inner skin of Shontay's slender thighs, "this pussy is so wet for me. I'll bet you want me to kiss it . . . and lick it . . . as much as I want to."

"Unhhh! Oh . . . yes . . ." Shontay gasped, twisting, looking down her long, thin, undulating body at Laura crouched between her thighs.

"Too bad we have to be so quiet," Laura murmured. "I'd love to suck this beautiful pussy until you scream."

"Oh god . . . we can't make any noise!" Shontay keened, suddenly panicking. "If anyone knew we were doing this . . . oh god!"

It was true. They were very vulnerable to being overheard. It wasn't as if total strangers inhabited all the other rooms along this corridor. They were fellow workers, 'colleagues,' supervisors and vice presidents. To overhear two of their number lecherously rutting in the next room, gasping and squealing and shuddering through the beautiful, intense orgasms Laura and Shontay were capable of giving each other, would be a source of endless amusement and salacious gossip for years to come.

Moreover, Shontay, being an executive director, had much more to lose than Laura did. She also had a hard crust exterior she showed constantly to the world, which she was clearly not eager to have penetrated. Finally, the fact that they were having a torrid lesbian encounter could not fail to raise eyebrows and cause months of prurient titillation.

"Don't worry," Laura smiled up at her reassuringly, parting Shontay's wet pussy lips with the fingers of both hands, exposing the glistening magenta flesh inside. "I'm going to make you come so softly you won't even know it's happening until it's over. Just grab one of those pillows if you feel like moaning too loud, okay?"

Looking like a frightened animal—but also a beautiful woman consumed by fierce sexual excitement—Shontay nodded. She reached one long arm up behind her and pulled down one of the pillows, leaving it close to her head.

In truth, though, Laura was wondering too how she could make Shontay come without unleashing a gusher of helpless moans and shrieks. Shontay was one of those women who did not come easily. She required absolute concentration and focus, and very great patience from Laura, to get to the finish line, and often by the time she got there her physical tension was so supreme that when her climax finally erupted, there was no way she could restrain her piercing cries.

But even though it was daunting, Laura wasn't going to let that stop her. It had taken a lot of anguish on both sides to reach this point in their relationship, and now that Shontay had surrendered once again after an initial resistance, Laura was not about to spurn the offer of this beautiful, long, angular body, or the sweet, sensitive, vulnerable girl who was offering it.

Holding Shontay's small, slick, oozing pussy open with her thumbs, she began slowly to lick the wet, exposed, inflamed cleft sensually with her tongue, starting at the bottom and ending at the top by wriggling the tip of her tongue up under the little hood that sheltered Shontay's tiny clit.

"Oh! Oh!" Shontay gasped, her pelvis jerking up excitedly. "God . . . I don't think I can be quiet!"

"Mmmm, yes you can," Laura purred, now burrowing her tongue into the juicy warm pit. "Just tell me if it gets too intense . . . then I'll slow down."

"Oh! I don't want you to slow down! It feels so good!"

For the next two or three minutes Laura was very careful and Shontay very silent, though the sexual tension was building gradually and relentlessly. Laura did not want it to go too fast, and Shontay was incapable of exploding without warning anyway. Often she shook and strained and mewled for several minutes before erupting. She quivered and mewled almost inaudibly while Laura luxuriated in the opportunity to lick her beautiful wet quim to her heart's content. Finally, Shontay's clit began to swell and become more visible, and Laura could not keep her tongue from sliding over it too.

"Oh!" Shontay gasped, her body clenching now more frequently. "Ohhnnnn!"

Laura found herself recalling her old apartment, and how she had struggled countless times to keep the neighbors from overhearing her cries and those of her climaxing lovers. The last neighbors upstairs, whom she had taken pains to guard from these ecstatic screams, were Shontay's own parents, though they had always been gone when Laura and Shontay had fucked, often heatedly, once after a ferocious cat fight, fucking savagely and sweetly on the floor in Shontay's own parents' apartment. It was hard not to remember it all now as she patiently, carefully, tenderly, then more passionately, licked the wet, shiny, bright magenta insides of the lovely, complicated girl's gorgeous, small, festering pussy, bringing low, guttural moans of pleasure from deep in Shontay's chest.

"Unnhhhh . . . unhhhh . . . unhhhhh Laura . . . ohnnnnn!"

"You're going to come . . . you're going to come, aren't you . . . darling . . ." Laura murmured to her, not really knowing if she was yet, since you never knew with Shontay until it actually arrived, but hoping to encourage her, build her confidence, get her to the pinnacle by cheering her on.

"Oh yes . . . oh yes!" Shontay whimpered, twisting, her beautiful, thin, honey-gold, long body writhing and her small breasts sliding up and down on her chest.

"You missed me, didn't you . . ." Laura chuckled softly. "You missed me sucking and licking your pretty pussy like this, didn't you?"

By now Laura was being much more adventurous, sucking Shontay's clit, hood and all, into her mouth, swirling her tongue around it, kneading Shontay's pretty, smooth little buns with her fingers.

Shontay's body suddenly clenched in a noticeable spasm, and she immediately began churning and panting faster. "Oh god, I think I *am* going to come, Laura! Yes! Oh shit . . . right there! Yes! Right there! Ungghh!"

Laura wanted her to come, but the closer they got, the more frightened she became of the consequences. It was a terrible dilemma. She wanted to pour it on about now, to give Shontay what she really needed to reach an obliterating orgasm of the kind Laura had given her countless times in the past. Shontay had become almost addicted to the way Laura often slid one long forefinger up into her ass just before she came, igniting exuberant firestorms of coming in a girl who had known nothing but her own tame, masturbatory orgasms before Laura came into her life. She craved it and would beg for it. It was, Laura reflected, about as kinky as they had ever become together.

Shontay was close to losing all control, and yet Laura, who knew she couldn't risk the finger-up-the-ass this time—it was way too dangerous—could not resist slipping one of her fingers between Shontay's smooth, tight little buns and pressing her fingertip against Shontay's perineum, the small area of skin between the lower part of her cunt and her asshole, a very sensitive spot, Laura knew.

"Ahnnggmmiiee!" Shontay cried out, her body almost jackknifing at the touch, her cry much louder than anything Laura had elicited from her so far.

"The pillow, honey . . . the pillow," Laura coached her softly, reaching up with her free hand and pulling it closer to Shontay's face, which was already torn by a grimace of piercing sexual feeling.

"Oh . . . oh yes! Unhhhhh!" Shontay panted, now swirling her hips, pushing her pussy up into Laura's mouth.

This was, to Laura, a very good sign. She's close. She is going to make it . . . any second. Now Laura began to massage Shontay's perineum while sucking and tonguing her pussy even more heatedly, though well aware that any instant she might have to take quick measures to muffle the girl's helpless screams as Shontay's long body began undulating more rapidly, and her breathing became more labored.

"Yes, honey . . . yes, honey . . . I'm going to suck your beautiful pussy so hard . . . you're going to come so hard . . . I'm going to fuck you so hard . . ." Laura murmured, knowing also that even though she would deny it, Shontay got aroused by having Laura talk dirty to her while fucking her.

Now Shontay began straining, and small, tortured, cawing sounds fought their way of her throat as her flesh clenched and stiffened. Laura had seen this before and was briefly discouraged. Often Shontay would nearly come and then for some reason fall back, as if getting to the peak were something she could not permit herself, as if there were obstacles that even she could not overcome.

But Laura had helped her overcome them dozens of times in the past, and now she only redoubled her efforts, half-gratified anyway that it wasn't going to end too soon, that she still had plenty of time to slurp this delicious small wet black pussy she was so hungrily devouring. The warm, thick nectars that flowed from Shontay's inflamed slit were tangy and tart and sweet and buttery all at once, and Laura drank them, grunting and snuffling almost comically herself with fervent lust as she rubbed Shontay between her anus and her pussy more and more insistently, and lashed Shontay's nearly-bursting clit with her tongue.

"Ungghh . . . ungghhh!" Shontay groaned, tossed her head, her body again jerking upward at the feel of Laura's finger pushing ever more sharply against her perineum.

"Oh yes . . . it's coming, honey . . ." Laura panted to her, sucking her clit, swallowing her sweet juices, now so in tune with Shontay's surging, pulsating flesh that she actually could feel the moment when Shontay finally arrived. "Oh god . . . it's now, baby!"

She didn't need to tell Shontay. Fortunately for them both, the first lightning bolt of Shontay's orgasm struck her so severely that the breath totally left her lungs. Only a tiny, hysterical squeaking could escape from her throat as her long, gangly body stiffened and then collapsed in spasms. This momentary silence gave Laura the opportunity to slide up Shontay's body, while replacing her tongue with her finger, thrusting it up into Shontay's clasping pussy and fucking her rapidly with it, as she covered Shontay's mouth with her other hand and held her, hearing the cries explode from deep in her chest.

"Awwoommnnnnggg!" Shontay groaned loudly into Laura's palm, her body jumping and straining as each fresh spasm wracked her. "Unnggmmm!"

A wrenching, crushing orgasm roiled inside her, and she lay twitching and shuddering through it for almost half a minute. Laura held her and kissed her smooth cheek and waited. Finally, it began to release its grip on her.

Laura was briefly alarmed that Shontay's cries were too loud, but before she could grab the pillow and turn Shontay's face into it, they began to subside into long, tremulous sighs of pleasure. The undulations of her body began to slow too, and the fluttering of her eyelids grew still. Laura held her, removing her hand from Shontay's mouth now, but still gently moving her fingers inside the warm, greasy folds of Shontay's still-throbbing pussy, unwilling to let the smallest twinge of pleasure die away.

After a few seconds of truly intense moaning and thrashing together on the bed, they were silent. The room was silent. It was quiet enough to hear their breathing, slowly returning to normal. It seemed like an eternity to Laura before Shontay turned her head and smiled wanly, her magical pale brown eyes still pulsing with the afterglow of this thrilling climax.

"I don't care how much you hurt me, I guess I'll always come back," she confessed in a hushed voice. "I don't think I could ever come like that in my life unless you did it."

"What a thing to say," Laura teased, acting mildly shocked. She wiggled her finger inside Shontay's warm pussy and watched Shontay's magical eyes roll up briefly. "One, I never tried to hurt you. Two, you might come even better with someone else, if you tried it."

Shontay shook her head solemnly. "I don't think so. And you do hurt me. You hurt me when you ignore me."

This was unpleasant information, though Laura could hardly act as if she didn't already know it. She was already so aroused from bringing Shontay to a stupendous orgasm and trying to make sure they weren't overheard that her mind could barely concentrate on Shontay's so typical complaints.

"I . . . I've been . . . very distracted lately," she stammered apologetically. "I . . . got hurt very badly myself."

At first Shontay looked curious, then pained. "Welcome to the club," she smirked, unable to repress a smile as she said it.

Laura removed her fingers reluctantly from the girl's warm, buttery slit. Shontay instantly recoiled.

"Don't touch me with that shit!" she half-giggled, trying to pull away, though Laura wouldn't let her. "Eeeewwooo . . . you're fingers are all wet!"

Laura smiled in wonder. She couldn't get over the squeamishness some women had about their own love juices. "You made it," she teased Shontay, glad to have a reason to change the subject. She waved her shiny wet fingers in Shontay's face, threatening to touch her with them. "It's your pussy juice. I love it. Watch."

Sensually, she wrapped her tongue around her two fingers and licked them clean.

"Yum. You have a delicious pussy, my dear. Why are you so afraid of this yummy nectar?"

Shontay frowned at her playfully. "Since you like it so much, you can have it all."

Laura was still holding her close, preventing her escape with one arm. She wiped the spittle off her fingers on the edge of the sheet. Then, turning to her most sultry, submissive manner, she cuddled closer to Shontay.

"Make love to me, honey," she whispered. "Make love to me. Make me come. Just put your hand down there and let me kiss you while I'm coming so I don't scream."

Shontay softened. A tiny smile again tugged at the corners of her mouth. Her pale brown eyes suddenly swirled with flecks of scintillating sexual fire.

"You sure?" she murmured, bringing one hand up to Laura's naked breasts, caressing and squeezing them, twisting Laura's nipples gently in her thumb and forefinger. "You don't want me to eat your pussy? You have a pretty nice one too, you know."

"I do want you to," Laura nodded. "But I want to kiss you and look into your eyes. I want you to look into mine and rub me and make me come. You can eat me when we get home."

"Mmmm," Shontay half-purred, dropping her mouth now to Laura's nipples, teasing and licking them. "Who said we're going to do this again when we get home?"

Laura didn't want to answer. She didn't want anything to get in the way of this pleasure, which seemed to grow and swell by the second. For all their checkered relationship and mutual suspicion, she and Shontay had been making love for months, and Shontay knew what it took to ring Laura's bells. Her mouth on Laura's breasts had Laura climbing the walls very quickly.

"Oh . . . god, that feels good!" Laura breathed, looking down at Shontay's wet, pink tongue dancing over her stiffening coral-hued nipples.

Shontay sucked each one slowly, skillfully, passionately, stopping only when Laura began lowing and groaning softly, twisting, pushing her pelvis forward into Shontay's body, giving every indication that she would not last much longer and desperately needed Shontay to bring her off.

"Oh god, you're killing me, I need it . . . I need it!" she whimpered into Shontay's hair, again delighting in the way it fell in messy, sexy clumps around Shontay's cheeks and forehead.

Shontay lifted her head, smiling, still massaging Laura's saliva-wet breasts with her fingers, now scissoring Laura's erect nipples between her long slim fingers. "I wish I could come as fast as you do," she whispered, her light brown eyes swirling, pulsing.

The sexual spell they had cast together now swept away Shontay's resentments, and she was totally caught up in the heat of the moment, as Laura was.

"Kiss me, you idiot," Laura panted, half-smiling. "You sex maniac. You rapist. Kiss me and fuck me with your hand."

Shontay's magical pale eyes flickered with mischief. "What if I don't?"

"Oh god, please," Laura panted, her face contorted by fierce need.

"Mmmm, I love you to beg me," Shontay said, kissing Laura's neck, breathing in her ear, sliding one long, graceful hand down Laura's body to her crotch, which was so hot and wet it was nearly steaming.

"Unhhhhh!" Laura gasped as she felt Shontay slide two fingers up into her squinchy wet furrow.

Shontay pulled her face out of Laura's hair. "You smell so good, Laura," she whispered, her breath now coming faster too. She looked seriously, almost solemnly, into Laura's eyes. "You've got to be quiet too."

"Oh! Oh! Oh god . . . it feels so good . . . just like that, yes!"

Laura began to gyrate her hips in slow, sensual fuck-rhythm, feeling Shontay's long slender fingers slide in and out of her sopping wet pussy. Shontay knew the effect her hand was having on Laura, and she was quickly drawn into the whirling vortex of Laura's gathering need, moving her fingers faster, letting the bottoms of them slide across the throbbing nub of Laura's clit, even clutching Laura's body harder against hers with her other arm.

"Laura . . ." she panted, now fucking Laura's pussy so hard and squirming together with her that the bed began to squeak. "You can't make any noise!"

"I know!" Laura gasped, pressing the full length of her body into Shontay's warm flesh, feeling her damp nipples slide against Shotnay's stiff little buds, jamming her crotch down into the girl's thrusting hand. "Unhhh! Ungghh! Oh!"

"Laura!"

"Auunngghh!"

"Laura . . . the pillow! Here!"

For all her concern about protecting them from the consequences of Shontay's potentially loud orgasm, Laura when it came to her own seemed to lose complete control. She knew it was dangerous, she knew she must control her moans and her cries, but somehow the moment— this delicious connection with Shontay in her bed after so much pain over Sara and so much distress at feeling Shontay's rejection—was piercing and sweet and overwhelming all in the same instant. She wanted to scream with joy as she felt the hot, rushing jolt of a surging orgasm begin to fill her body.

"Here!" Shontay almost shouted again, snatching the pillow that Laura had earlier pulled close for her to use, and pushing it into Laura's face, forcing it between them, just as an ear-splitting, helpless cry of thrilling rapture ripped its way out of Laura's throat.

"Owwmmmnngggwwoommmmmoouunngghh!" Laura screamed into the pillow, her body stiffening, then collapsing into several sharp spasms as a stirring orgasm wracked her. "Unnmmmgghh . . . ohngghhh!"

After a few seconds, she turned her face aside from the pillow to breathe as the intensity weakened, and her moans grew correspondingly softer. Her hips were still undulating and quivering, and she could still feel Shontay's two fingers sunk deep inside her pussy, and Shontay's long arm wrapped around her back, pulling her close. As Laura's groans subsided into panting, Shontay pulled the pillow away.

"You didn't get to look in my eyes, like you wanted," she whispered, kissing Laura's cheek. "You can look in them now."

"Oh god, I think I could have another one, if you just hold it like that!" Laura gasped, knowing with some mysterious certainty that she was poised on the edge of a second climax.

Looking into Shontay's pale eyes, so adoring, so soft, smoldering with so much sex and affection and sensuality, made it even more certain.

"Are you really going to come again?" Shontay asked softly, as if unbelieving.

"I . . . think so," Laura panted, again pushing her throbbing pussy down into Shotnay's hand. "Look at me . . . look at me . . . and fuck me . . ."

"Like this?"

"Oh god, yes! Unhhhh! Oh god . . . yes, right now . . . it's—"

This time she was not so afraid of screaming and merely pushed her face into Shontay's smooth shoulder, squeaking and mewling as a fresh orgasm streamed through her body like a radiant wave, filling her flesh with warm honey, then melting into small feathery spasms that seemed to last an eternity. Shontay held her throughout, then kissed her gently on the face as Laura began to recover.

"I'm so envious," she murmured, seriously, kissing Laura's forehead, finally removing her fingers from Laura's wet pussy. She wiped them, trying to be surreptitious, on the sheet. "Not only can you come so quick, you can also come twice. Like at the same time. First one, then another. God, I've never done that."

"Did I make too much noise?"

Shontay broke into a grin. "You were trying. I nearly suffocated you with that pillow to get you to stop."

Laura nodded. "You did. I guess it was necessary. I don't know what came over me. Just having you . . . hold me like that, and doing everything to me . . . and I just came and I couldn't help screaming."

Shontay loved this praise and nearly blushed herself, looking down momentarily. "I guess I'm getting it right."

Laura embraced her ardently, and kissed her sensual mouth hungrily. "I guess you are."

They dozed dreamily, nestled together, for a long time. Laura luxuriated in pushing her face into the messy clumps of Shontay's hair, inhaling the clean, somehow sexually stirring, odor of her scalp, and the musky perfume that now seemed to wreathe her skin as the consequence of their sweet coupling. She knew she probably smelled the same way to Shontay.

"I'm beginning to want you again," she murmured drowsily into Shontay's molasses-colored ear, slipping her tongue inside of it.

Shontay giggled softly and squirmed free. "Laura! We can't. It's bad enough we did it already. What if somebody heard? Do you know who's in these rooms next to you?"

Laura shook her head. "We were quiet enough. Don't worry."

Now that she had thought of it again, Shontay seemed very nervous. Laura tried to calm her.

"I want your body," she murmured, kissing Shontay's long, smooth, golden neck. "I want to push my pussy into your pussy."

Shontay squirmed again, this time not so much out of nerves as renewed sexual excitement. "We can't. Wait until we get home."

"You said we might not be doing this when we get home," Laura smiled, feigning petulance, pouting.

Shontay softened. "I can't . . . stop wanting to," she confessed. "I told you . . . I never came that way except with you. I can't stop wanting it."

Even though Shontay looked like she wished she *could* stop wanting it, Laura understood. "Great. Then, when we get home, we have a big fucking party at your place. How about it?"

Shontay frowned. "You're making fun of me."

"Am not," Laura grinned.

"Are too." Shontay cocked an eyebrow. "Why can't we have it at your place? Have you got something to hide?"

"Only the depths of my lust for your wonderful sexy skinny body," Laura laughed, dragging her down on her back on the mattress and swarming all over her in a passionate fever of mock lechery.

They laughed and rolled around tickling one another for about a minute, until the bed began to squeak. Then it seemed to occur to both of them at the same instant that they might be overheard having this tickle mania moment. How ironic to be caught playing when nobody overheard us fucking like two lust-crazed minks only a few minutes ago, Laura thought. She could see from Shontay's eyes, even though her face was contorted with suppressed laughter, that she was thinking the same thing.

They had rarely if ever shared such a relaxed, playful moment. Laura wondered if Shontay had ever shared one with anybody. It brought a new intimacy into their relationship, a deeper emotion that now made them both more reluctant to part. And yet Laura knew in the back of her mind that if she were not feeling so bereft of Sara, she would not be feeling this deep tug of emotion for Shontay.

"I have to go back to my room," Shontay said, sitting up, looking around the room for her bathrobe.

"I wish you would stay here," Laura purred, trying to pull her down to the sheet again. "We could sleep and, you know, cuddle and . . ."

"That's just the problem," Shontay pulled away. "I can't control my feelings." Her eyes sparkled at Laura, and she gave her a small, reluctant grin.

"You mean you want it like I do," Laura said.

Shontay nodded, but in the next moment she got up from the bed, found her bathrobe crumpled on the floor, shook it out, and slipped it on. "I've got to go back. In the morning there will be more people in the halls. They'll see."

"I know," Laura admitted.

It was the right thing to do. She couldn't deny it. She waylaid Shontay at the door. They kissed, softly, romantically.

"I had fun," Shontay whispered.

"Me too," Laura winked. "Sleep tight."

But after Shontay had left, Laura could not sleep herself. Boy, 'fun' doesn't even describe it, she thought. That was intense. She is a very intense woman. I mean, we just diddled a little and each of us came . . . but it was emotionally intense.

She switched on the small TV in the corner and realized after a few minutes that it had been the wrong thing to do. On the old movies channel, *To Have and Have Not* was playing, starring Bogie and Lauren Bacall. Laura recalled Sara having told her that if she had been born white she would want to look like Lauren Bacall. "Sorry, Laura," she had said, with her usual sardonic wit. "You're second."

The memory was piercingly sad to Laura, who sat up watching the movie until one o'clock, trying to pay attention to it without thinking of Sara.

* * *

HOT LESBIAN EROTICA

La Chatte Noire

THE LAURA AND SHONTAY CHRONICLES, PART 3

Miranda Mars

There was an uncomfortable shock in store for Laura.

She was in ninth heaven after her night with Arthell, which helped to cushion the blow a little, though not much. While lying in bed with Sara on Friday night, in Sara's apartment, tired and happy after an hour of intensely sweet and tender fucking, Sara grew solemn. Tracing an invisible line down Laura's cheek with one finger, her dark eyes wide and limpid, she asked,

"Would you hate me if I did this with another woman?"

When Laura, who was floored by the totally unexpected question, failed to answer right away, Sara went on. She even kissed Laura's mouth, half-open with awe and shock, first.

"Don't be upset," she whispered. "It wouldn't mean I didn't love you. I know how upset you were when Evangelina paid me that visit. Even though she and I are old friends. You see it didn't affect the way I feel about you." Sara's fingertip made a curve under Laura's chin and up her other cheek. "And I know you haven't been exactly . . . how shall we put it . . . chaste? I don't mean just Dee Dee. But I'm not blind. I can sense when you've been . . . you know, sniffing some other chick's crotch."

She made one of her devastatingly funny faces, which, in spite of her stunned silence, made Laura laugh. It was a gesture that made it absolutely impossible for Laura to lie and protest that Sara's accusation was not true. She considered it the better part of discretion to remain silent.

But when Sara did not go on, Laura said, "I wouldn't hate you. I would never hate you."

"I hope you mean it," Sara said softly.

"Why. Have you done it already?"

Sara shook her head, looking suddenly very innocent and shocked to be suspected. "Only with Lina. I mean, Evangelina." She propped her head on her hand, gazing intently into Laura's eyes. "There's this nurse who works down at 450 Sutter, across the hall from my office. We meet in the hallways, in the elevator, down at the snack shop, you know. She's been sort of, well, you know, coming on to me. It's kind of getting under my skin, if you know what I mean."

Laura nodded sympathetically, not knowing what else to do. She was both pained and fascinated by Sara's account of this attraction. "And you want to give her the green light? See what happens?"

Wide-eyed, Sara slowly nodded. "She's kind of pretty. Not as gorgeous as you are, but . . ."

"Is she white or black?" Laura blurted out before she could catch herself. "Or Latina," she quickly added, remembering Evangelina. Or 'Lina,' as Sara had just called her, revealing a level of intimacy that Laura had always expected was there but that hurt just the same when she was reminded of it.

Sara frowned, not a deep frown but a frown nonetheless. "Why? Does that matter to you?" Then she made a dopey face. "Are you that competitive, Laura?"

Laura blushed. "I . . . guess I am. Sorry."

"Lucky for you, she's a sister." Sara raised one eyebrow. "Knowing you, she'd probably turn your crank."

"Now that's not nice," Laura smiled. "She obviously turns yours."

Sara smiled mysteriously back at Laura. "I guess in a way she does."

Laura recognized this moment as a time when she could pout and turn petulant, perhaps playing on Sara's clear uneasiness at broaching this question. She decided not to do it. *After all, you haven't been a saint,* she reminded herself. *You love her, and you know fucking with the others hasn't made you love her any less. Why shouldn't it work for her? In spite of the fact that I'm wildly, murderously jealous?*

"What's her name?"

"None of your business," Sara turned away, as if to brush off this inquiry quickly.

"You mean I don't even get to know my rival's name?" Laura asked querulously, caressing Sara's bare brown shoulder. She realized she was skirting perilously close to the pouting she had foresworn.

"She is *not* your rival!" Sara said, angrily.

"I know . . . I'm sorry," Laura said, pulling her down again on the bed, running her hands hungrily all over Sara's wonderful curvaceous body, even though they had finished fucking only minutes earlier.

She realized that Sara's attraction to another woman suddenly made her somehow incredibly more desirable than ever to Laura. Her body felt suddenly new, fresh, alluringly voluptuous under Laura's fingers, her scent outrageously erotic, her skin a magnet for Laura's hungry lips. In another second, she had Sara's phenomenal breasts in both hands and was attempting to swallow one of her large, soft black nipples.

"Oh! Oh! Laura!" Sara hammered her fists on Laura's shoulders, half-laughing, half overcome by this sudden sexual attack.

"No wonder she wants this delicious body," Laura panted, slurping and sucking Sara's silky dark flesh with exaggerated lust.

"Oh honey . . . oh honey . . ." Sara panted, converting quickly from protest to participation.

Laura realized, and knew that Sara probably did too, that sudden, explosive sex was one way to veer around the dangerous and complex emotions their conversation had been inspiring in them both. In another minute they were deep into it, gasping and pumping and pinching and sucking, until both of them erupted more quickly than usual in sharp, squealing orgasms that left them exhausted and panting, oblivious to their earlier troubled sparring.

"Sometimes I can't believe you," Sara finally said, when she recovered her composure, rolling over to kiss the supine Laura's bare shoulder. "Nobody ever fucked me like you do."

Laura gave her a deadpan smile. She too leaned over and kissed Sara's phenomenal pillowy lips. "Let's just make sure we keep it that way," she murmured. "You might have an occasional dalliance, but I want to still be the champ."

"Nobody could ever replace you in my heart, Laura," Sara whispered solemnly.

But Laura could not help wondering.

She knew it was silly, but she worried anyway, until an email came at work that distracted her. It was from, of all people, Shontay Gibson.

Hi Laura, longtime no see. Coming to San Jose week of Oct. 4 to recruit for Alcatel. Staying in Radisson Suites. Can we visit? Dying to see you. It's been so long. Shontay. Write back here and let me know.

Laura felt her heart flutter and tiny hot darts raced through her pussy. It was not that Shontay was so important to her, certainly not as important as Sara. Or now, Arthell. But their relationship had been fascinating and dangerous and passionate, and Shontay, always jealous, had left to take her job in France with Alcatel without the slightest word to Laura. She had disappeared without notice and without a trace, with not so much as a fare thee well, leaving Laura to wonder what might have caused this vanishing act, and if she herself were partially to blame.

That had been about eight months ago, and Laura had heard nothing until this email. Feeling very excited, though Shontay's visit was still two weeks away, she immediately replied that she was looking forward to seeing her. She wanted to ask, What do you mean by Can we visit? She was totally in the dark about where their relationship stood. She and Shontay had gone so often from eating one another alive to frosty distance to actual spite and then back again to hot fucking that it was really hard to know where they would pick things up. At the time Shontay had vanished, they had been embroiled in a jealous spat, caused, as always, by Shontay's anger at Laura for playing around with others.

Do we pretend that didn't happen? Laura wondered. Am I going down to the San Jose Radisson to spend the night? Or just to make polite conversation?

She didn't know and was on pins and needles until the evening of the fourth, when she received a call from Shontay at home.

"Hi, I'm here, when are you coming down?"

"Oh god, Shontay, it's really you." Laura flushed, and found herself momentarily speechless. "You really are here."

"Of course I'm here," Shontay said, a little curtly. "Did you think I was lying?"

"No. No, I just had a hard time believing I was actually going to see you again."

"What's that supposed to mean?" Shontay snapped.

It was the same old Shontay, Laura realized. Very touchy, edgy, easy to ire, no matter what you might venture to say. Laura paused for a moment, hoping Shontay would hear the sound of her own sharp voice and soften a little.

"It's supposed to mean," she finally said, "that I'm dying to see you. I can come whenever it's convenient for you."

Even though it was an obvious compliment, Shontay did indeed seem to soften, as if she realized she was being a little harsh for someone who wanted to 'visit'. "I'm sorry, I'm a little frazzled from that long flight," she said. "I didn't mean to snap at you. I'm going to try to get some sleep, but I'll probably be up by two a.m. My internal clock hasn't adjusted yet."

"I'm afraid I can't come at two. I have to go to work tomorrow."

"Why don't you come down now? I know I won't be able to sleep."

Laura felt her whole being suddenly come alive. She had been tired herself, but no more. Her body suddenly perked up and almost vibrated. "I could be there in an hour or so. I don't know how exactly how long it would take to drive there."

"It shouldn't take you long. Come the back way, down 280."

"Right. Want me to bring anything? Food? Wine? Champagne?"

"You know me. I don't eat much. Wine will just make me sleepy. Just bring yourself. And bring the Laura I used to know . . . back when we had the good times. See you in a half hour or so."

Laura was positively humming as she packed a small suitcase.

This love of mine,
Goes on and on,
Though life is empty since you've gone . . .

She didn't know why this tune stuck in her brain. She certainly had never 'loved' Shontay, at least not in the way she adored Sara, or had felt such deep emotion for Deshona at one time. Or even the way she felt now, all tingly and ethereally happy, about Arthell. Shontay however had felt more strongly, she knew, since that was the source of their frequent quarrels. Life had not been exactly empty for Laura since she had gone to France, though. It had rarely been more exciting sexually, though the recent development with Sara (*that slutty nurse Sheena*, as Laura thought of it) had put a damper on it.

Still, she hummed the tune and packed in her strap-on just in case, and a small bottle of baby oil.

I cry my heart out,
It's bound to break,
Since nothing matters, let it break . . .

"Why am I singing this song?" she wondered aloud. "I've never felt happier. Even with Sara doing . . . her little thing. In a way, it makes me feel relieved since I don't have to feel guilty for being the only one doing it."

She realized she was talking to herself and promptly stopped. But she couldn't stop humming as she locked up the house and went out to the car. She hummed all the way to San Jose. *Do you know the way to San Jose? I've been away so long I may go wrong and lose my way.* She did not lose her way and arrived at the Radisson Suites in 47 minutes. Shontay was waiting for her in the lobby.

Laura was shocked. Shontay was gorgeous.

Laura knew she was pretty and had been the one to encourage Shontay to see herself that way, since Shontay had been convinced that, being tall and skinny, she was unalterably homely and unattractive. And she had dressed accordingly until Laura had persuaded her to wear silky, summery things that showed off her long but enchanting legs and her willowy figure. She had usually worn her hair too either in a tight bun behind her head or in a no-nonsense pony tail, but never down around her neck and cheeks, where it softened her somewhat angular face and made her look like an aristocratic and elegant model. Laura was continually taking down Shontay's hair, mussing it up, or asking to do so.

But here she was in the lobby, wearing a stylish peach-colored frock with a short skirt, with her lovely dark brown hair in soft billows around her head, her astonishing pale brown eyes lighting up with genuine gladness as she saw Laura approach.

"Oh god, you look so gorgeous!" Laura effused as she hugged her, inhaling Shontay's French perfume. "France must be so good for you."

Shontay giggled nervously and stepped back from Laura's embrace, as if this were too public a place for them to be doing something they would be doing behind closed doors in a few minutes. "Oh, cut the crap, Laura," she smiled. "We both know what you want."

Laura glanced around the lobby without moving her head, mainly to see if anyone had overheard this. She smiled sweetly back at Shontay. "I want to hear all about it, that's what I want. You do look gorgeous. I hope you won't deny it."

"You don't look too bad either," Shontay softened. "Still got all that hair."

Laura raised her hand to her hair self-consciously. She was still taking in the vision of Shontay's loveliness. Shontay was still almost painfully thin, and still looked like she had no breasts, though Laura knew otherwise. The flowery peach dress she wore did not allow one to appreciate the fine curve of her delicious rump, though Laura also knew it well. But her long thin legs were visible from the hem down and Laura's eyes feasted on them.

Shontay was the color, Laura had often though in the past, of pale clover honey, her skin smooth and flawless, and Laura could well recall having been locked between those long smooth legs, rubbing her cheek against them, kissing Shontay's inner thighs . . .

These thoughts were getting her aroused right there in the lobby, and she quickly pushed them to the back of her mind. Suddenly she found it a little awkward to be standing there in the lobby, not knowing what was coming next. It somehow didn't seem appropriate to her for them just to go up to Shontay's room and fuck. Assuming that was what Shontay had in mind. But it seemed too coarse and perfunctory.

"Shall we go have dinner . . . or a drink?" Laura suggested. "So you can tell me about it?"

Shontay scowled. As usual, Laura reminded herself, even when she was in the mood, Shontay had to scowl or snarl or make a sharp comment. She was very vulnerable and sweet inside, but outside she kept up her aloof, imperious, peremptory façade, which was a quality that had made her much disliked when she had worked at Laura's company. Laura wondered how Alcatel was handling the famously frosty Shontay. Maybe the French language softens her for them, she speculated. And then, she is a gorgeous black American model type; they probably go for that. Maybe it induces them to tolerate this crabby nature of hers. Or maybe she's not like that at all when she's around them. Only around me, and others like me.

Then Shontay's scowl turned mysteriously into a seductive smile. "I'm tired," she said quietly. "Let's go upstairs. We can order room service. Company's paying," she winked.

"I'd be delighted."

Shontay looked down at Laura's bag. "Planning to stay over? They might charge me extra." She winked again, clearly meaning it as a joke.

"I don't have to stay if you don't want me to," Laura said softly as they entered the elevator.

They were alone in it, and Shontay's room was on the twelfth floor. She did not answer Laura's question, letting it hang. Finally, she looked back over her shoulder as she led Laura down the hall to her room. She was grinning.

"I'll let you know."

Inside the room Laura sat on the edge of one queen-sized bed and kicked off her shoes. Shontay went over to the drapes and pulled them shut. Gosh, we aren't going to waste any time, are we, Laura thought. She realized she was very aroused. She knew Shontay, though skinny and sharp, always had this effect on her, probably because of the challenge involved in breaking through the ice layer. She was also physically lovely, though skinny. You could still be lovely while skinny. Laura's eyes lingered on the smooth, rich café-au-lait hue of Shontay's long legs.

Shontay saw her looking and smiled. "You know, I think you're the first woman who ever found me attractive," she said calmly.

"But not the last," Laura smirked knowingly.

Shontay shook her head. Her loose hair swished around her ears, making Laura's pussy flutter. "No, not the last. I've got two lovers in France. Girls. Actually, three. One guy, if you can believe it. They're wild for *la chatte noire*, as they call it."

God, I could use a little of that *chatte noire* myself right now, Laura thought, feeling very aroused, very hungry for Shontay. The new Shontay, she corrected herself. Once Laura had broken through the ice, Shontay was always eager for fucking, except when she was periodically furious with Laura over Laura's other girlfriends. But prior to Laura, she had, as she recounted it, simply given up on sex, with men of course, since Laura had been her first woman.

And now look at her. Not only gorgeous, stylish, self-assured, and sexy, but possessed of three, count them, three French lovers of both sexes.

"I'm a little wild for it myself," Laura said, unable to resist the opportunity.

"I know," Shontay said mordantly. "Black cunt."

She was alluding to one of their conversations long ago, when she had accused Laura bluntly of being overly fond of this lovely item. Hers and others'. The words 'black cunt' sounded so earthy and coarse and dirty coming from this gorgeous woman who looked like a supermodel that the combination was enchanting, and Laura perceived her lust ratcheting up a few notches. Black cunt sounded so much more arousing than *la chatte noire*. Though maybe the latter sounded pretty sexy if you were French.

"You're so nasty," Laura smiled curtly. "Always so nasty and rude. You meant way more to me than . . . that."

Shontay tossed her head in an arrogant, aristocratic way she had. She pursed her lips. "I doubt it."

Laura pouted. "You didn't even tell me before you left. I had to find out from that bitch Rhonda."

Shontay looked away as if embarrassed. Laura felt a slight twinge of victory. "What did she tell you?"

Laura shrugged. "That you got a job in France. That you spoke French and had graduated from the French high school in San Francisco. I felt . . . devastated."

"Oh, right," Shontay said, with heavy scorn.

Maybe that was a little too strong, Laura realized, and as ever Shontay was quick to jump on any phoniness. "Well . . . I *was* hurt," she amended.

Shontay grinned broadly. "Poor Laura. You had to go back to the pretty airheads. Boo hoo."

"I think we are on the wrong track," Laura said, frankly, looking directly into those enchanting pale brown eyes. "I came here because I missed you. You invited me, remember? If you think all I want is *la chatte noire*, then maybe I ought to leave."

Shontay softened again, as she usually did. Laura recalled that you had to work at it constantly, but you could get her to relax and drop the shield. But Shontay was not done teasing, in her sharp sarcastic way. She didn't want Laura to leave, but she also did not want to stop baiting her.

"Oh, and you don't want me?"

"More than anything," Laura said softly.

This was such an odd change, Laura realized. She had initially had to convince Shontay that she was indeed attractive, not the gawky, spindle-shanks, skinny, awkward, angular woman she had thought herself to be, and now Shontay was acting like a very sexy and desirable woman, toying with Laura, tempting her, taunting her, and enjoying Laura's eyes on her and Laura's obvious desire enough to prolong things with agonizing skill.

Shontay crossed the room and sat next to Laura on one of the two beds. She reached up with one hand and let her fingers trail through some strands of Laura's hair. "You know," she murmured in a very low voice, almost too low to be heard, "I really love my French girls, and the guy too, but none of them can do it for me like you did, Laura."

"I thought the French were experts in love."

Shontay let her fingers caress Laura's cheek. "Maybe in love . . . but not in . . . you know . . . that word you like so much that I told you embarrasses me."

"Fucking?"

Shontay giggled and flinched. "That's the one. I think I've missed you, Laura."

Slowly, Laura pulled her backward down onto the bed, so that they were both lying half on it, with their legs still dangling over the edge. "God, I've missed you too."

"I don't want to wrinkle up this dress," Shontay said. "I'm traveling. I only have so many. And I don't trust any hotel's cleaning service."

"I know what you mean. Why don't you let me help you take it off?"

Without answering, with only a mysterious smile, Shontay slowly sat up and turned her back to Laura. There were four buttons on her dress, which Laura unbuttoned, starting at the top. As each button came loose, and the thin fabric of Shontay's dress sagged away from her flesh, Laura kissed her smooth light brown skin, holding up Shontay's hair with one hand so that she could reach the nape of her neck with her lips.

Shontay shivered a little. She raised her own hand to her hair and held it up so that Laura could continue.

"I could kiss your marvelous back forever," Laura whispered, continuing with the buttons.

Shontay was not wearing a bra but an ivory-colored thin camisole, where Laura's lips had to stop, even though there were two buttons left. But she was content for the moment. She was a great lover of naked backs, or near-naked ones, and Shontay's was enchanting, even if

Laura had to stop momentarily halfway down. True, the wings of her shoulder blades protruded a little, and the knobs of her spine were a little more visible than most, a feature Shontay herself would consider 'bony.'

Maybe her back had a little less flesh on it than many others, but it was the color of pale honey, silky and smooth, and had a lot of seductive cambers and indentations and dips and protuberances to kiss and tenderly suck, and even though inhibited from going lower for the moment, Laura's lips were busy visiting them all.

Shontay was enjoying it too. "Oh god . . . that feels good," she sighed, bending her head forward a little to give Laura full access to the nape of her neck again.

Laura took advantage of the opportunity and licked and sucked the skin sensually. She then kissed the slightly raised nub of each vertebra on her way again down Shontay's back to the edge of the camisole. Meanwhile, she was unbuttoning the last two buttons. Shontay's dress now gaped open, and Laura could reach the bottom of the camisole with her fingers.

"Here . . . let's take this off," she murmured, pushing the top half of the loose dress down Shontay's arms, then lifting up the camisole, with Shontay's help.

Shontay turned to face her as the camisole went up over her head. When it came free, she was naked from the waist up. Laura's hands were already covering the marvelous little teacup breasts that she remembered so well. Her mouth came close to Shontay's, then pressed into it, and they were kissing hungrily.

Shontay's long arms encircled Laura, and her fingers plucked at the fabric of Laura's shirt. "Take this off," she breathed into Laura's lips.

Laura pulled back, smiling. "Let's take everything off."

Shontay shook her head. "No. A little bit at a time. More exciting that way. The way you used to do it." She watched while Laura unbuttoned her shirt, removed it, then removed her black lace bra too. "Remember when we were fighting . . . and you pushed your mouth into my panties? Pushed my panties up into my . . ."

Laura waited, still smiling. "Your pussy? Can't you say that? Your *chatte*? You're beautiful *chatte noire*?"

Shontay looked down, in genuine embarrassment. It was such a thrill for Laura to see her like this since she was always so sharp and imperious. She did have a streak of genuine vulnerability which was however hard to reach. But this moment also reminded Laura how Shontay had quickly become much more emotionally invested in their relationship than Laura had been, which had caused their frequent hostilities.

"Let me feel you," Laura whispered, holding out her open arms again. "It's been so long."

Shontay nodded slowly, leaning forward, coming into Laura's outstretched arms. Now their naked breasts touched at the same time their mouths met, and they melted together into a lengthy, sensual kiss, moving their half-naked bodies together so that they could feel every last bit of pleasure from their skins touching, their breasts rubbing together, their hardening nipples kissing too.

Laura ran her fingers now up and down the whole supple length of Shontay's marvelous long back, feeling the smooth skin that had formerly been concealed by the camisole, wanting to kiss it, feeling the sexual pressure build inside her body, surprised by the physical desire she had for this thin, complicated girl.

"Mmmm, I want to kiss this incredible back forever," she purred, rubbing the warm, smooth skin and long resilient muscles. "Lie down and let me rub and kiss your back."

Obediently, Shontay quickly shed the rest of her frock, wriggling out of it and tossing it across the room onto a chair. She still had on her ivory bikini panties, which matched her camisole. She stretched out on her stomach, looking dreamily back over her shoulder as Laura began making love to her back.

There was no other word for it. Laura loved this honey gold masterpiece. Now that Shontay was completely naked, except for her panties, Laura could explore, caress, and kiss it to her heart's content. She began by slipping out of her own skirt so that she too was wearing only her panties, then straddling Shontay's long, thin thighs with her own and massaging the firm flesh on each side of Shontay's neck, starting gently, squeezing the muscles, then doing it a little harder, until Shontay was gasping and moaning.

"Oh god, I love your back . . ." Laura murmured, bending close, letting her own naked breasts sweep across the flesh of Shontay's back as she pressed her lips to the firm flesh she had been rubbing. "I love your body. I missed this long thin body so much."

Shontay was sighing and moaning almost unconsciously. Her eyes fluttered open and she smiled drowsily. "You liar," she sighed softly. "If you keep this up, I'll fall asleep and there won't be any fun."

Laura leaned up a little further so that her lips could reach Shontay's ear. Her breasts now mashed more forcefully into Shontay's naked back, and she slithered her tongue into the marvelous molasses-colored whorl. "There's going to be fun you wouldn't believe, darling," she breathed. "You didn't know I'm the jealous type. I'm going to put those French girls in the shade."

Shontay shivered and giggled throatily and writhed a little under Laura's body.

"And if you fall asleep, I know just how to wake you up."

"I'll bet you do," Shontay smiled.

She tried to turn and get up to face Laura, but Laura was having none of it. "I'm not finished. Lie still. I haven't even got down half of this incredible back."

For the next five minutes Laura explored every silky inch of tawny, honey-colored flesh on Shontay's back, working from the top to the bottom, kissing and rubbing and stroking Shontay's long, smooth muscles, until her lips finally reached the wonderful shallow dimples above the girl's delicious, up-jutting bottom. For a tall, thin woman, Shontay had, as Laura had remarked in the past, a spectacular ass. Apart from her singular aloof and imperious beauty, the first thing Laura had noticed about Shontay was this magnificent little rump, which had been clearly visible in its outlines even under the drab, severe business pants suits Shontay had always worn until Laura persuaded her to give them a rest.

It was high and firm and out-curved, the way Laura loved them, not large, not pendulous, but a high, tight little butt that Laura just ached to kiss, stroke, and bite. And now she had an opportunity again to do just that. She knew it had driven Shontay wild in the past, and she intended for history to repeat itself.

"I love your ass," she murmured, pulling Shontay's panties down to reveal it. "God, I love your ass."

Shontay said nothing but squirmed a little with her hips to lift her ass up even more, knowing how besotted Laura always was with it. Laura had pulled Shontay's panties halfway down her thighs and decided now just to take them completely off. She kissed the upper slopes of Shontay's buns while doing it, then flung them off the bed and passion-ately attacked Shontay's beautiful bottom for real, squeezing and sucking and kissing Shontay's firm golden cheeks until Shontay was gasping and wriggling.

"Oh . . . oh . . . oh god, Laura . . . oh god that feels so good . . . oh yesssss!"

"I love your ass," Laura panted. "And I love your sweet pussy . . ."

She couldn't keep her hand off it. Even though she was mouth-mauling Shontay's beautiful ass, she dipped one hand under it and rubbed the wet, swollen lips of Shontay's pussy with the tips of all her fingers. Shontay undulated under her caresses, panting more and more uncontrollably. Suddenly, she twisted her body and sat up, forcing Laura to the side, so that they were again face to face.

"You . . . don't get to have all the fun . . ." she panted, her marvelous pale brown eyes fiery and glazed.

"I thought you *were* having fun," Laura teased.

Shontay grabbed her forcefully and pulled Laura down on the bed with her. "I am. I want you too. I didn't call you up just so you could . . . do that. I want some too. I want your body too."

Laura smiled warmly at her. "So nice to be wanted. I suppose you want me to get out of these."

She pointed to her own panties as she slid them down off her legs. Shontay watched intently, then purposely put her hand between Laura's thighs, as Laura had done to her, a shocking gesture from the usually shy and somewhat inhibited girl. The new Shontay, Laura thought. Aggressive. Knows what she wants.

"That's better," Shontay murmured, still touching Laura's wet pussy, but with her other arm encircling Laura's neck, bringing her face close for another hot, wet tongue kiss.

They started slowly, kissing sensually and rubbing each other's pussy gently, though insistently, but the heat level slowly grew until they were groping harder and sucking each other's lips, clanking teeth, panting and mewling. Both were so wet and aroused that Laura wondered how either one could last another minute. She herself was notoriously quick to come at a moment like this, the first time, when they had both just got naked and were groping and sucking and rubbing together. But Shontay was different—or at least she had been in the past—and rarely came quickly or easily.

At the moment, however, it seemed like she might come at any second. Low, helpless gurgles of sexual excitement came from deep in her throat as Laura massaged her swollen, greasy cunt with two fingers, swirling them over Shontay's clit, which she knew was a tiny pinkish jewel and still hidden under its protective hood. Laura had sucked and tongued this pussy she was rubbing so many times in a rapture of wild sexual worship that she knew it well, and was loving the process of getting reacquainted.

"Unhh! Ungghrrrmmm!" Shontay half-growled, her body sagging momentarily in Laura's embrace.

But even though they both seemed to be close, there was always a part of Laura that didn't want it to happen fast. She loved holding Shontay's thin, angular, naked body against hers. She loved the feel of Shontay's small but very firm breasts pushing into her own excited flesh, and she was hungry to get her mouth once again on those marvelous quarter-sized dark caramel nipples. She wanted to taste the wonderful flavors of this delicious small slit she was now rubbing heatedly. She knew there would be time, there would be time enough for all of this, but she somehow wanted it all now, as usual succumbing to her impossible desires, her need to consume and ingest and inhale her present lover.

"Unhh! Ungghrrrmmm!" Shontay groaned again, this time a little more desperately.

"Oh god . . . honey . . . I think I might come!" Laura gasped into her cheek, letting her mouth fall to Shontay's bare shoulder, nipping it lightly in her frenzy.

Shontay was similarly overcome but not so lost that she couldn't smile mysteriously down at Laura and move her hand more swiftly in Laura's crotch. "Good," she panted, "do it."

"Ohhhnnngggg!" Laura gasped, feeling it arrive whether she wanted it yet or not. "Oh god . . . unngghhhh . . . aauunnnggghhhh! Mnnnnggggauugghhnnn!"

She couldn't stop herself and came in a quick, wrenching spasm that threw her body off balance so that she fell to the mattress, pulling Shontay down with her, straining and shuddering through the last few jolts. Miraculously, her hand was still fastened to Shontay's pussy, and she rubbed it again excitedly.

"Want you to come too . . ." she gasped into Shontay's shoulder. "Want you to come."

"Oh!" Shontay gasped, thrusting with her hips. "Oh . . . unnnn! Laura . . . yes!"

"Are you there?"

"Oh! Oh . . . almost," Shontay grimaced, pumping hard, her fingers biting into Laura's arm. "Unnngghh!" she groaned, her face contorted, her body hard and tense.

For some reason, Laura was flooded with a fresh influx of sexual frenzy, probably from knowing that she was about to make Shontay come. There was a shiny spot of her own spittle left between Shontay's wonderful honey-gold shoulder and her neck, left there when Laura had bitten it just before coming herself. She immediately opened her mouth and sucked this piece of Shontay's flesh back into it, sliding two fingers up into Shontay's inflamed wet pussy and fucking her frantically with them. Next she sucked her way up to Shontay's long, smooth, aristocratic neck, then to her earlobe, which she nipped lustfully.

"Oh god, I love to fuck you!" she whispered, remembering how dirty talk had always ignited Shontay's most violent orgasms.

Shontay's thin, long, flexing thighs clenched a little, and her body jumped in a sharp spasm. "Anngghiiee!" a tight squeal escaped from her throat.

Laura, knowing she was coming, pinned her to the bed, rolling on top of her and hand-fucking her relentlessly. Another hard flinch, and then Shontay went into quick, spastic convulsions, whinnying softly deep in her chest. Her long, angular body undulated under Laura's, and her muscles contracted in a rolling rhythm of quick orgasmic fluttering.

"Oh! Ohhnnnnnnn! Ohnnnnnn . . . god, Laura, god . . . ohhnnnnnn!" she moaned, clenching, sighing and gurgling for a long minute, then coming out of it almost as quickly as Laura had come out of her own climax.

Laura's had been quick and explosive, while Shontay's had been rolling thunder, but both were humbled and stunned by the aftermath, and they melted together effortlessly, sighing and laughing softly and stroking each other as the sweet waning spasms died away. Laura kissed her neck again, and her shoulder, and licked them both, unable to get enough of this rich, smooth, tawny golden skin.

"My, that was quick," she murmured, still half-breathless, into Shontay's delicious, silky, honey-colored throat.

"I think it was a record for me," Shontay grinned, also panting softly, kissing Laura back on her forehead. She yawned. "You'll have to forgive me if I fall asleep. Long flight. Jet lag."

"I'll bet I can keep you awake," Laura nuzzled her, dropping her face down Shontay's smooth upper chest to her marvelous little teacup breasts, which she was not going to deprive herself of any longer. "For a while, at least."

Shontay smiled drowsily, watching Laura's tongue snake out to lick one of her beautiful bulging caramel nipples. "I forgot how you like to rut and rut."

"You mean fuck and fuck?"

"Whatever. Ohhhhnnnn . . . god, that feels good. Do the other one too?"

"Mmmm, like this?"

"Yesss!"

Laura treasured these beautiful little mounds and made love to them both with exquisite skill, licking and tonguing Shontay's dark, thick nipples, then sucking and even nipping them, until they were stiff and rubbery and wet and shiny like dark plums, darker now that she had been sucking them and drawing blood into them. She slid up to kiss Shontay again while pinching Shontay's wet nipples with her fingers, scissoring them lightly, twisting them, squeezing the girl's small breasts and slithering her tongue deep into Shontay's mouth.

"Are you going to let me fuck you again before you fall asleep?" she teased, nibbling Shontay's earlobe. "You love it when I talk dirty to you, don't you."

"Oui, mademoiselle," Shontay smiled sexily, drowsily. "I love it when you 'fuck' me . . . and also when you tell me you're going to 'fuck' me."

As always, Shontay was very skittish about using the 'F' word and isolated it playfully from the rest of her words for Laura's benefit. "Baise-moi," she said, saucily, looking as if she might blush, if only she were pale enough to blush. "Baise-moi vite."

"Oh god," Laura erupted in soft laughter, "am I getting my French lesson for today? Mademoiselle Dupin, my tenth grade French teacher, would never let us use that word. Anyway, doesn't it mean 'kiss'? Kiss me?"

Shontay gave her a salacious smile. "It means kiss me and fuck me."

"You know," Laura said, "I brought along a little surprise. I don't know if you'll go for it . . . but . . ."

She hopped off the bed in a fit of happiness and enthusiasm. Shontay was so different: so receptive, still a little sharp, it was true, but mainly sweet and sensual and beautiful and relaxed with Laura. Was this what having three French lovers could do for you?

Laura popped across the room to her small overnight bag and extracted the strap-on dildo. She had not brought the Double Penetrator, feeling that was a little overboard for a woman to whom she had never even broached the subject of a strap-on before. Just the single ridged brown beauty that could take you to paradise when fastened to the right person.

Shontay looked at it with wry curiosity as Laura returned to the bed with it. "Oh god, I can't believe it. You really have one of those. Excuse me, I *can* believe it."

Laura presented it, so that Shontay could run her fingertip along the ridges. "This will make you die, honey."

Shontay gave her a quizzical look. "Are you going to use that on me?"

This was not the way Laura would have put it herself, and Shontay's attitude suddenly made her feel chagrined. She pulled back the dildo slowly, winding the harness straps around it as if she were preparing to put it back. "Not . . . necessarily," she stammered. "I mean . . . of course not if you don't want to."

Shontay realized that she had somehow embarrassed Laura. In the past she might have gloried in this opportunity for scorn, but now she was more pliant and warm. "Let me see it again."

She held out her hand. Laura put the dildo, wrapped in the harness straps, into it. Shontay unwrapped it and caressed it again, this time more fascinated than semi-appalled. "You know . . ." she said, almost hesitantly, as if she were being careful not to hurt Laura's feelings. "Like I told you, I have this guy in France. Named Michel. He . . . you know . . . does me like that. Whenever I let him. It isn't really what I was looking for with you."

Laura smiled and reached out to take the dildo back. "I understand perfectly," she said. "It was only a thought. Shoot, I just enjoy kissing you. And pushing my body against yours. I don't need this thing. It was just a passing idea."

She crossed the room and put it back into her small bag. When she returned, Shontay had uncoiled her long, lanky, thin, and to Laura gorgeous light brown body, so that she was stretched out full length across the bed, from top to bottom, propping her head on one hand, smiling at Laura in a mysterious way, her phenomenal pale brown eyes flecked with glowing embers of sex that Laura remembered seeing there in the past. Her hair, earlier in soft billows around her head and cheeks, was now mussed and askew and fluffed out, making her look wildly sensual and fiercely desirable to Laura.

"Let me tell you something," Shontay murmured, as Laura rejoined her on the bed, stretching out to face her, but scooting up too, since Shontay was about four inches taller than she was. "You know what I keep remembering? That time when we did it in my Daddy's armchair. Remember that?"

"How could I ever forget it," Laura rolled her eyes up. "I don't think I've ever had such a hot experience."

Shontay laughed. "Me either. I couldn't look at that chair afterward. Every time I would visit them, I'd just have to keep from looking at it. Or if I were there alone, feeding Willie [her parents' cat], I'd just act like it didn't exist. You know, make wide circles around it, while looking up at the ceiling. I was afraid if I looked at it, I start creaming my panties, or panting, or whimpering, or something."

Laura leaned forward and kissed her, a long, romantic, tongue-entangling kiss. "Do you feel like you want to do that again?" she whispered.

Without answering, Shontay let her eyes drift across the large hotel room to the easy chair by the window. It was a taut, upholstered maroon chair with sturdy thick arms. The instant Laura saw it she realized that it might be even better for the purpose than Mr. Gibson's worn overstuffed monster where they had first done this.

"I'm only afraid I'll scream so loud that the hotel staff will try to break in to save me," Shontay confessed charmingly.

"Mmmm, we can probably come up with a solution for that," Laura said, scooting forward as she kissed her again, so that she could feel the entire length of their naked bodies pressing together, a sensation that always made her head suddenly light.

Now that she knew their ultimate destination, Laura could take her time. She knew what Shontay wanted, she knew where they would end up, but for the moment she could take her pleasure with Shontay's marvelous, smooth, slender body. Shontay rarely came quickly anyway, and certainly not the second time, so that Laura could make the most of this opportunity and bring the girl to the absolute brink before dragging her across the room to the chair for a final loving rape.

"Are you going to let me suck your beautiful pussy first?" Laura murmured against her soft light brown cheek. "Such a beautiful pussy . . . your little *chatte noire*, and you waste it all on those lucky French girls and that guy Michel, when here I am dying for it . . . dying to slide my tongue right up into it . . ."

While she was murmuring softly to Shontay, she was also descending with her mouth and hands down the girl's long, angular, naked body, nuzzling her flesh, sucking her dark caramel nipples again, still descending, kissing every inch of Shontay's long midriff, every silky soft ridge of long muscle, every inch of smooth, downy skin, every rise of surfacing rib, until her lips reached the upper edge of Shontay's raven-black pubic patch, which she felt bristling against her chin. The ripe, musky perfumes of Shontay's aroused cunt filled her nostrils.

During this slow descent, Shontay sighed and twisted, growing more aroused the lower that Laura went, knowing her ultimate goal, knowing that this was only preliminary to Laura's mouth on her pussy, driving her to new heights of need. She said nothing but looked down her long body at Laura's mouth on her flesh, at Laura's tongue burrowing into her navel, at Laura's fingers gently pinching and kneading her erect nipples.

"Ohhhnnnn! Unhhhhh! Ungghh!" she finally groaned as Laura's lips reached the swollen, spreading petals of her gaping pussy.

As Laura now remembered, though everything about Shontay was long—her arms, her legs, her waist, her glorious back, her entire body—and her skin was the color of pale sage honey, her pussy lips were actually very black, and her pussy itself was small, not long at all, a snug little glistening magenta slot, all juicy and wet inside, her labia swollen and gaping. Laura wasted no time in pouring her worship all over it.

She sucked and tongued and licked it for about five minutes, at first going slowly, not wanting to accelerate Shontay's arousal too quickly, instead letting it percolate and simmer, avoiding Shontay's clit until the later stages. Finally, with her thumbs she spread open the small hood concealing the magic bead, which in Shontay's case was tiny but extremely sensitive. Laura licked it carefully, watching Shontay's face as the girl grimaced with pleasure and whimpered.

"Unnhhhh! Oh! Unnhhhh . . . oh Laura!"

"Mmmm, I don't want you to come yet . . . because I'm going to fuck you in the chair. Remember?" Laura murmured softly to her, taking great care now not to arouse her past the breaking point, though she knew it was unlikely Shontay would come too fast.

But this calculation proved to be premature. After passionately licking and sucking Shontay's small, beautiful pussy for three or four minutes she realized that Shontay was getting close, very close, far closer than she had expected. Shontay whimpered, mewling softly and help-lessly, her hips swirling, her pelvis occasionally quaking, her fingers flut-tering around her nipples, then twisting them absently as she gasped, her bleary eyes rolling upward. Laura could recognize the signs, and the last thing she wanted—and she knew the last thing Shontay wanted—was for her to come before they got over to the chair. There were, after all, a finite number of orgasms they could have, especially when Shontay was so exhausted and jet lagged, and they both yearned for that one.

Laura pulled back, not abruptly, not wishing to disturb the flow of Shontay's increasingly urgent sexual rhythms, but slowly, kissing her tense thighs, then her smooth, flat belly, sliding upward until she held her and they were face to face.

"Come with me, ma cherie," she murmured to her, kissing her cheek, her ear. "Come with me to the chair. Laura is going to fuck your pretty pussy to heaven."

Shontay's lovely pale brown eyes were glazed, her breath coming quickly, her mouth slack, but she managed a wry smile. "Oui . . . made-moiselle," she said, her eyelids heavy, quickly sitting up and following Laura off the bed as Laura pulled her by the hand.

They crossed the room to the chair, which Laura tugged out a lit-tle from the wall to make it more accessible.

"Laura . . . I'm going to scream. I know I am," Shontay said again. "I'm so damned horny, even after that first one. God, you got me all worked up, girl."

"Don't worry about a thing, darling," Laura reassured her, turning her and placing her in the chair. "I'm going to kiss you so hard you can scream right into my mouth. No one will hear a thing but me. And I *want* to hear it."

Since they had done this before, though months earlier, Shontay knew how to place herself, and Laura only had to assist her. Shontay lay back in the chair at nearly a forty-five degree angle, with her magnificent tight little rump perched on the very edge of the cushion, her lovely small black pussy splayed and inflamed and upturned, the wet red inner flesh raw and shiny with juices. Her amazingly long legs she propped over the arms, spreading her thighs so widely that it was the easiest thing in the world for Laura to climb on top of her and straddle the arms of the chair with her own thighs, also spreading her own groin enough for her throbbing cunt to press directly down onto Shontay's.

The sensation of their wet, warm, raw inner cunt flesh touching sent them both into temporary paroxysms of sexual pleasure.

Shontay stiffened and shuddered a little. "Unhhhhh! Oh shit . . . oh merde!" she giggled. "I forgot how good that feels."

Laura leaned forward and placed both hands on the back of the chair, remembering how this gave her almost ferocious leverage for fucking. This could be sweet, could be gentle, but it was likely to be fierce and explosive instead, as it had been last time. After they had done it in Shontay's father's chair, Shontay had accused Laura, though playfully, of having raped her. She had of course enjoyed the entire ride, and she appeared to be enjoying this one too.

"Unhh! Unhhh!" she grunted softly as Laura, now beginning to move her body up and down, slid her pussy across Shontay's slippery, gaping little slit.

"Ohhnngg!" Laura groaned, throwing back her head.

She too had forgotten the sheer intensity that this position could summon. With her arms extended over Shontay's head, her hands gripping the back of the chair, her naked breasts swished in Shontay's face. Shontay's hands quickly came up to them, as she had done their first time, squeezing Laura's breasts and immediately feeding one of Laura's aching nipples into her mouth. She sucked it hungrily.

"Auunngghh!" Laura half-growled, hissing with sharp pleasure. "Oh yes!"

For a brief few seconds which seemed elongated and stretched out into long minutes, they slowly moved their wet pussies together while Shontay sucked Laura's nipple as well as a large chunk of Laura's small breast entirely into her mouth, holding it there while they rocked slowly together, their hips gyrating in perfect union, slowly and patiently and relentlessly. Oh god, it's going to be even better than the first time! Laura thought wildly, feeling her body course and throb with fire and complete yearning for this magnificent, thin, and temperamental woman.

She buried her face in Shontay's frazzled, fluffed up hair, inhaling the clean, sweet odor of her scalp, gasping as she felt the slippery flesh of their cunts sliding together, intermingled with their tangled crotch hair, their clits occasionally rubbing in a way that made them both wince.

"Ungghhhh . . . oh god . . . I forgot how much I love to fuck you, Shontay . . ." Laura panted, pushing her tingling breast hard into Shontay's face. "Suck it hard. Harder!"

Shontay, while groaning and whimpering as Laura jammed her cunt into her crotch rhythmically, was also making sloppy, wet, sucking sounds as she slurped and mouth-mauled Laura's nipples, and somehow these wonderfully obscene noises ratcheted up Laura's lust to an even higher notch. Her nipples were on fire, and she even dropped one hand from the top of the chair to Shontay's head, pulling it from behind, forcing Shontay's mouth even harder into her breast.

"Bite it . . ." she gasped, losing control briefly, consumed by the fiery urge to obliterate them both in a volcanic uprush of coming. "Oh yes . . . auunngghhh!"

Shontay would bite, but never very hard, as Laura knew. She let her teeth sink a little more into Laura's throbbing nipple, then a little more, and Laura suddenly realized that if they kept this up she herself was going to come in seconds. Just in response to Shontay's teeth she was rearing and gurgling and digging her fingers into Shontay's silky flesh, groaning and at the same time fighting back the surging waves of an inevitable orgasm.

Oh no! Not so fast . . . not so fast! she told herself, wrenching herself back into self-control, slowing the pace dramatically.

"Oh noooooo . . . I don't want it to be over," she moaned to Shontay, pulling her breast out of Shontay's mouth, leaning down to hastily kiss her forehead, now glowing with a thin film of sweat. "I don't want it to be over too fast!"

Shontay, eyes glazed, smiled up at her dreamily. Without replying, she began undulating her pelvis again, so that their pussies again pressed together. Her pale brown eyes held Laura's, solemn and deadly serious, as if this moment of intimacy were the only thing that mattered in the universe at this instant. Finally, she managed to control her rapid breathing enough to speak to Laura, a soft, labored gasp.

"I . . . don't . . . either," she panted.

For Laura at least, this was the point at which the emotional content of their encounter began to deepen and expand. Something about Shontay's eyes holding hers like that stirred awake in them both a recollection of the deeper, complex feelings they had once had for each other, never 'love' in any real sense, but certainly a kind of fierce attraction-repulsion that was in some ways deeper than love. In the grip of this sudden spell, they had slowed the tempo of their fucking down to a careful, patient grind, which had the advantage of making each minuscule sensation magnified and piquant, so that the slipperiness of their wet pussies sliding together now filled them both with an almost unbearably emotional as well as sexual pleasure.

For the moment Shontay had stopped sucking Laura's breasts, which however still dangled in her face. Instead, she reached up with both hands to hold them, still never letting her eyes leave Laura's. For several minutes they gyrated together, and the only sound in the room was the chuffing of their labored breathing. But their feelings seemed to throb and swell and pulse as much as their bodies, and Laura could not prevent herself from momentarily stopping their slow grind to lower her mouth to Shontay's and drink it thirstily.

It was hard to thrust while they were kissing, but Shontay started moving her hips again in the middle of the kiss, and Laura responded, gyrating back. This quickly became so arousing that they had to stop kissing, and were panting hard, but Laura's face was still close. Shontay reached up with one hand, dropping one of Laura's breasts, and spread away the filaments of Laura's hair that had become stuck to her sweaty forehead. It was a very tender gesture that wrenched Laura's heart, so frequently had they fought and snarled at each other in the past.

"Are you going to 'fuck' me, mademoiselle?" Shontay whispered hoarsely, her pale brown eyes now flecked with excited sparks, swirling and pulsing, as if she were not going to last much longer and was asking for the final stroke. "Baise-moi? Are you going to rape me, like before?"

Laura smiled, panting seriously now. "Is that what you want me to do?" she gasped in a hoarse whisper of her own.

Again not letting Laura's eyes leave hers, Shontay nodded slowly. "I think I'm pretty close."

"God, I know I sure am," Laura gasped, kissing her again savagely before beginning to accelerate their grinding and slow pumping.

They knew they were both heading for the same goal, and that it was very close, which encouraged them to pour it on, and they began fucking more energetically and roughly than they had up to now. Laura pushed her slippery wet pussy down sharply into Shontay's inflamed seam, grunting softly and jabbing forward with her hips, grabbing the back of the chair hard for leverage, fucking her like a man would fuck her, roughly, hungrily, demandingly, completely.

For her part, Shontay, though whimpering and mewling and definitely the one underneath, who was being the recipient of this fierce love assault, flexed her body and gyrated her cunt up into Laura's too, meeting each of Laura's thrusts with her own, gasping and groaning as their physical struggle became almost too intense for either of them to bear. Now she had both hands again on Laura's small, swirling breasts, squeezing them, then voraciously feeding Laura's nipples, first one, then the other, into her mouth, sucking them sharply, deeply.

"Unnnunnnn . . . unnnunnnnn . . ." Laura heard herself moaning, her voice sounding completely demented as she pushed her breasts into Shontay's face and rabbit-jabbed the girl's warm, runny pussy with her own oozing slit. "Ohhngg! Yesssss . . . bite it . . . yesss! Unngghh!"

"Aunngghh! Oh god . . . Laura!" Shontay gasped, her thin, angular body arching and quivering under Laura's, as if she were losing control.

"You're going to come now . . . you're going to come . . . now . . . now . . ." Laura panted deliriously to her, leaning forward, but still thrusting and pumping more wildly than ever, grunting, digging her fingers into the upholstery of the chair, jamming her cunt into Shontay's, feeling her own climax surge up inside her body. "Now . . . now . . . you're going to come now . . . NOW!"

"Yaaunngngggg!" a savage, clotted cry tore itself out of Shontay's throat.

In the space of a few seconds her long, lean body went stiff, then went crazy, flipping and jackknifing almost off the chair. Laura, who was coming herself, was barely able to keep their bodies from separating, but she did it by dropping her arms from the top of the chair and embracing Shontay with them hard, mashing their bodies together, then shuddering and undulating herself as a soaring, gushing explosion of an orgasm wracked her own flesh.

"Ohnnnnmmmnngggg! Auunggghhhhh!" Laura groaned, shaking and clenching as a supreme climax wrenched her body almost too much for her to enjoy the cataclysmic nature of Shontay's.

For a moment it sounded to her like they were giving each other a chance to yell. After Shontay's initial outburst was ripped from her throat, she went silent, except for furious gasping and panting. Her body was gripped by fierce convulsions that precluded anything but mute expressions of deep physical rapture. The first jolts of Laura's climax shook and throttled her, but soon waned enough for the agonizing groans of release that had just flowed out of her lungs to surface. As they began to die away she remembered that Shontay had feared crying out too loudly, and that she herself had promised to prevent it.

"Oh honey . . . oh honey!" she gasped, grabbing Shontay's lolling head in both hands and pushing her mouth into the girl's just as Shontay erupted in a piercing scream of ecstasy. At least it would have been piercing, Laura knew, had it issued directly into the hotel room, but instead it was blocked by her open mouth. She swallowed Shontay's screams of pleasure, and for Laura it somehow made the entire experience more intense than ever, as if she were swallowing Shontay's orgasm at the same time that it was raking and wrenching Shontay's body.

"Mmmnnggrrrrnngghmmmnngghhbbrrr!" Shontay shrieked into Laura's mouth, her body still clenching and jackknifing as each shattering spasm of her climax ripped through her. "Aunnmmmgggh! Unnn-mmrrrggghhh!"

Just as quickly as her screams had arrived, they departed, slacking off into soft, helpless mewling. The fiercest moment was past. Since they were both having trouble breathing in this odd, bent position, and also in danger of getting muscle cramps from the violent jerking and flexing they had both been undergoing, Laura quickly pulled back and slid to the side, climbing awkwardly over one arm of the chair to give Shontay more freedom of movement.

But Shontay, though blasted and destroyed by her pulverizing orgasm, grabbed Laura's hand, looking up in a dazed, stunned way at her. "Oh no . . . don't leave me."

Laura smiled and stopped. She slid halfway back into the chair, again on top of Shontay, but pressing against her more gingerly now, and half-supporting herself on the chair arm instead of Shontay's relaxed, ravished body. "I wasn't going to leave you," she explained softly. "Just ease up so you didn't get a cramp. Or me, either."

Shontay smiled wanly. "Come here and kiss me. I don't care if I get a cramp."

Laura leaned forward and kissed her more lovingly than she believed she had ever done. The new Shontay. All hair-mussed and glassy-eyed and smiling dreamily after a stunning orgasm. Her long, smooth, light brown, angular body naked and warm against Laura's. Shontay kissed back with more emotion than before. Good thing you live in France now, darling, Laura thought, or we'd be right back into the thicket we were in before you left.

"You are so sexy," Laura whispered against her smooth cheek, "that I think I could come again if I could just lie stretched out with you on the bed. You know, before you go to sleep. I am such a greedy little pig for your beautiful body."

Ever flattered by Laura's praise of her thin, somewhat bony body, Shontay grinned and flirted. "You sure are," she laughed softly, tickled by Laura's frank lechery. "You already came twice."

"You inspire me," Laura nuzzled her long, aristocratic neck.

Slowly, they disentangled themselves and Laura helped Shontay up from the chair. Shontay began yawning before she was on her feet, raising the back of one hand to her mouth. "Okay . . . but I don't know if I can make it myself," she sighed, still half-yawning. "Two is about my limit. And I'm exhausted. You really raped me again."

Her eyes twinkled at Laura.

Laura drew her back over the bed, and they stretched out face to face on it. "I hope you don't think I forced myself on you," she teased.

Shontay smiled and caressed Laura's cheek with her fingertips. "You can rape me like that any time you get the chance," she whispered. "You know, I tried that with one of my girlfriends in France. Not the chair thing . . . but just pussy to pussy. We couldn't come. Either one of us. It was fun, though. But we couldn't come. I kept remembering, Shit, every time I did this with Laura we both came."

Laura thought about it a moment. "Maybe it has to do with the build-up. You know, how long it takes you to get there. What you do before. How wound tight you are."

"Probably," Shontay nodded. "Anyway, thanks. I really needed that. I'd been thinking about it for months."

"Me too," Laura lied. Though if she had known Shontay would reappear in her life, she might have been thinking about it, she reasoned.

"Really?" Shontay beamed.

Laura nodded. "I really missed you. I was very upset that you left without telling me."

A trace of the old scorn passed over Shontay's face. "A likely story. You were busy with that skinny teenager with the braids."

"She wasn't a teenager," Laura pouted. "I'm always perfectly legal."

"Liar!" But Shontay was smiling. In the past she would have been excoriating Laura on the spot for her various peccadilloes.

Laura pulled her naked body close again and playfully tickled her armpits. "When your hair gets all messed up like that, it just makes me want to fuck you forever," she breathed into Shontay's perfect light brown ear.

"I told you I can't come again. Too tired. But go ahead, do whatever it takes you to get off. I'm your slave for love. And lust. Just use me and let me fall asleep." She winked. "We can make it again when I wake up, which if past trips are any indication, will be about three-thirty a.m."

Laura's face fell. "You make me sound so . . . so disgusting and lecherous."

Shontay laughed, throwing back her head. "If the shoe fits . . ."

"All right, that's it. No more for you." Laura sat up and crossed her arms over her naked breasts. "I might not even be here when you wake up."

Shontay grinned and pulled Laura down next to her again. "Want to bet?"

Laura smirked and laughed, trying not to. "Kiss me, you angel," she murmured. "If you had been this nice a long time ago, the girl in the braids would never have caught my eye."

"Touché, mademoiselle," Shontay murmured back, again spreading the hair away from Laura's sticky forehead before kissing her very emotionally.

After the kiss they dozed and cuddled, and soon Shontay was actually asleep, as she had promised. Laura must have watched her for half an hour before nodding off herself.

~~The End~~

WANT FREE COPIES OF MY BOOKS?
Just visit my blog and download free copies of my books:
http://miranda-mars.awesomeauthors.org/

Here is a sample from another story you may enjoy:

INTERRACIAL LESBIAN SEX
MIRANDA MARS
Double Or Nothing
for Allisha

Makeeda would be gone in New Jersey, cutting her CD, for about ten days, and Laura, glowing with deep love for her, made an unwise secret vow to remain chaste during that period. It won't hurt you, she cautioned herself. You can practice fidelity and maybe get good at it.

But Shelley was too tempting. She too knew what it was like to have a lover far away. With Shelley, Laura had a deeply satisfying sexual relationship that did not threaten her feelings for Makeeda, and it was hard to renounce. She expected it to keep her well occupied until Makeeda returned, not counting on a ravishing young girl she began to see nearly every day on the Metro on her way to work.

At first, true to her vows, she tried to ignore the girl, who looked to be about eighteen or nineteen and was utterly gorgeous, so much so that Laura could not understand why everyone else on the rail car wasn't staring at her as much as Laura wanted to do but with difficulty refrained from doing. She had long hair, as long as Laura's (so unusual in a black woman), that was tastefully streaked dark honey gold. She had dark flashing eyes and smooth dark brown skin and a fantastically small waist, which accentuated the rest of her slender figure, her delicious bottom, her small breasts, her long thin legs.

She got on the Metro each morning when Laura herself did, at the Forest Hill Metro Station. She was very self-composed, dressed neatly and conservatively, and kept to herself, sitting almost primly in a window seat, and reading a small book. She was effortlessly beautiful and did nothing to call attention to herself, which only made her more desirable to Laura.

The Metro light rail car had a line of single seats along one side, where the girl usually sat. But one morning the single seats were full, and she was sitting on the other side, next to the window in one of the double seats. The seat next to her was— miraculously, Laura thought— empty. Laura mustered up the courage to sit in it.

"Hi," she said, brightly but softly, a friendly greeting but not so intrusive as to require anything but a smile in return.

Which was exactly what she got. The girl turned from her book and gave Laura a pleasantly blank smile, not even showing her teeth, her black eyes opaque and guarded, as most people's were on public transportation. Laura didn't blame her a bit. Ick, this stranger, being overly friendly. No conversations, please, the girl's eyes said.

But Laura realized that her own choices were limited. This was the first, and maybe the last, time a seat was available next to the girl. Makeeda would be out of town for another nine days or so. Laura knew she would not be able to make contact with this girl if Makeeda were home. She could not let this moment pass.

"I love your hair," she said softly, after a decent interval. "I keep looking at it every morning. It's so . . . unusual."

By this she meant that most black women did not have such long or soft or flowing hair, and not this rich brown color either. She knew that the girl understood exactly what she was saying, but now she could not help but feel self-conscious, as if she had strayed over the line and said something mildly racist or at least too familiar. But instead of growing more remote, the girl smiled more widely at her, this time showing her even white teeth.

"Thank you."

"Is that . . . the natural color?"

She shook her head. Her thick, beautiful hair moved. "My Mom's a beautician. She does it for me."

Laura smiled. The girl went back to her book. Laura didn't know how to resume. Anything she said now would seem too forward. She waited, nervous, pretending to read her newspaper, hoping something would happen to allow her to speak again. Finally they reached the Powell Street station. The girl made motions to indicate that she was going to get off and Laura should let her out of the window seat.

"Oh . . . this is your stop, isn't it," Laura said, quickly clutching her own bag and paper, standing. "I . . . have to get off here too today," she improvised. "I have to stop by Walgreens on my way to work to pick up something."

The girl smiled tightly, as if to say, I hope you aren't going to harass me any further with your pleasantries. They emerged onto the sidewalk walking next to each other, but the girl suddenly veered left.

"Oh . . ." Laura half-groaned disconsolately, unable to keep her disappointment from showing. "I was hoping . . . we could talk."

She hardly believed she had said this and began blushing almost the instant the girl turned, a few paces away, to face her again. The girl was smiling sardonically.

"Forgive me for being blunt," she said, "but are you a lesbian...?"

If you enjoyed this sample then look for **Double Or Nothing for Allisha.**

Also by this Author:

Deep Excavation

Chocolate Sandwich

Post-Game Specials

A Breach in the Preacher's Daughter

Deeply Detoured

The Rich Bitch Itch

"Hard" Competition

Little Rich Girls Go First

Superior Playmate

Spicing Up a Business Conference

Green Minds Lead to Colorful Results

Dirty Acquaintance

Menage a Trois

Provisional Test

Holiday Treat and Heat

Sex on the 46th Floor

Sneak, Peek and Squeak

Distance Leads to a Sexual Marathon

Confessions and Steamy Clinches

Screams of Pleasure

There, I've Said It Again...

There's No One But You

There Is No Greater Love

Sex Frenzy

A Rising Star

Raging Desire

It Hurts So Good

I Remember You

Don't Adore Me, Just...

Bittersweet Reunion

And Sheena Makes Three...

Gail's Awakening

We'll Be Together Again

Taneesha Wants Some of That

"Some Say the World Will End in Fire... Some Say in Ice..."

Reckless Betrayal

Please Take Me Back, Baby!

Play Coquette

Pervert Devotion

My Little Yoga Darling

Icicles Can Melt

Caught in the Act

Pull My Hair and Make Me Come!

The Emperor Wants Your Pussy!

Three on a Bed

No One Can Replace You

Lock Up the Dogs!

Not While She's Looking

Blindfold Me and Lick Me All Over

Do Me Up the Ass Please

Ride 'Em Cowgirl

I'm Going to Come So Fast

Gina Loves the Dick

Bathtub Sex With Frankie

Spanking Gina's Beautiful Black Ass

Finding Marni's G-Spot

Naked and Horny in the Woods

Marni Wants It Hard, Ashley Wants It Wet

Water My Ficus

Deshona Chronicles Compilation

Kissing Marni's Mom

Shagging Shamika's Aunt

Laura and Gail Chronicles

Laura and Frankie Chronicles

Laura and Arthell Chronicles Compilation

Laura and Makeeda Chronicles Compilation

Bonnie Chronicles Compilation

Drilling for a Filling

Bi-Curious: A Compilation

Revenge Is So Sweet

Double Or Nothing for Allisha

I Never Kissed a Girl Before

From the Author

WANT FREE COPIES OF MY BOOKS?
Just visit my blog and download free copies of my books:
http://miranda-mars.awesomeauthors.org/

If you'd like to give me comments or suggestions to any of my books, feel free to shoot me an email at: miranda_mars@awesomeauthors.org.

Check my page on Amazon and my blog for Updates and interesting info.

Author Central - http://amzn.to/14wSFHW

If you enjoyed any of my books then please share the love and click like on my books in Amazon.

If you write me a review and send me an email I will send you a free book, or many.
(Just know that these emails are filtered by my publisher.)

Good news is always welcome.

One Last Thing, For Kindle Readers...

When you turn the page, Kindle will give you the opportunity to rate this book and share your thoughts on Facebook and Twitter. If you enjoyed my writings, would you please take a few seconds to let your friends know about it? Because... when they enjoy they will be grateful to you and so will I.

Thank You!

Miranda Mars
Miranda_mars@awesomeauthors.org

About the Author

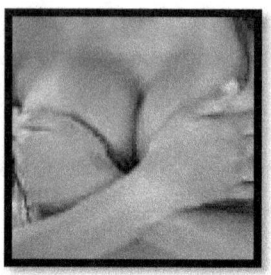

Miranda Mars lives with her cats and her exercise machines with her "special" friend in a suburb in San Francisco. Here is where she lavishly spends scribbling erotica for your, and her own, amusement.

She is especially attracted to dark-skinned women, and uses them as the lovers of the main characters in the stories she writes. She says they're just so hot! So dark-skinned women, BEWARE! :-)

Her stories are also surprisingly VERY ENTERTAINING for MEN!